Also by Janet McDonald

Harlem Hustle
Brother Hood
Twists and Turns
Chill Wind
Spellbound

OFF-COLOR

OFF-COLOR

JANET McDONALD

Frances Foster Books • Farrar, Straus and Giroux • New York

Distributed in Canada by Douglas & McIntyre Ltd.
Printed and bound in the United States of America
Designed by Irene Metaxatos
First edition, 2007
10 9 8 7 6 5 4 3 2 1

www.fsgkidsbooks.com

Library of Congress Cataloging-in-Publication Data
McDonald, Janet, date.
    Off-color / Janet McDonald.— 1st ed.
        p.   cm.
    Summary: Fifteen-year-old Cameron living with her single-mother in Brooklyn finds
her search for identity further challenged when she discovers that she is the product of
a biracial relationship.
    ISBN-13: 978-0-374-37196-8
    ISBN-10: 0-374-37196-2
    [1. Identity—Fiction.   2. Racially mixed people—Fiction.   3. Mothers and
daughters—Fiction.   4. Single-parent families—Fiction.   5. Interpersonal relations—
Fiction.   6. High schools—Fiction.   7. Schools—Fiction.   8. Brooklyn (New York,
N.Y.)—Fiction.]   I. Title.

PZ7.M4784178 Off 2007
[Fic]—dc22
                                                                              2006047334

TO MY AFRICAN-AMERICAN INDIAN MOTHER,

FLORENCE BIRDSONG McDONALD

ACKNOWLEDGMENTS This book would be an idea without my agent, Charlotte Sheedy, who carried it forth, and my keen and kind editor, Frances Foster, who flayed its flaws and sharpened its strengths.

This writer would be but a memory without the shock brigade that carried me forth to slay the dragon: Maria "Ange Gardien" Duarte, Paulette "Jane" Constantino, Annie "Cat" Gleason, "Maman" Françoise Greisch, Suzanne "Benzi" Banfi, Marie-Hélène Bérard, Shirl the Pearl Niel, Princess Marie Chicken-Oscar, Colette Modiano, "Trendy" Laetitia Perraut, Ginny "Queen of Queens" Power, Stéphanie "Petit Trésor" Rousseau, Marie-Christine DeLavergne, Olivia "Helpline" Sigal, Karyn "Massachusetts Lady" Korieth, Lynn "Astral Girl" Bell, Annabel Courage and Olivia Berthon, Lisa "Gallant" Hayes, Madina "Super Copine" Guillerme, "The Real Janet" Prata, Kokie "White Fang" Adams, Lillian "Sagesse Orientale" Ginoza, Myrianne Montlouis-Calixte, Gwen Wock, and Jemia LeClézio.

This sister would be alone without her brother Kevin "Project Boy" McDonald.

To you all, my deepest gratitude.

OFF-COLOR

The girl in the mirror shook her tangled dark curls and wiggled her narrow hips, lip-synching into a hairbrush. "Isn't anyone trying to *fiind meee*?" she mouthed, grimacing with passion. She tossed aside the improvised microphone to free her hands for a guitar solo. Sweat stained the armpits of her black "Enter at Your Own Risk" T-shirt. Her fingers danced wildly along the imaginary neck of an air guitar. Another sound caught her attention. She stopped for a moment and listened. Her mother's voice. Bummer. Why'd her mom have to hound her every single morning of every single school day? So she'd be a little late, so what. She continued her concert, grabbing the hairbrush just in time for the chorus. "It's a *daaamn . . . cooold . . . niiight!*"

The bedroom door banged open.

"*Cameron!*" Her mother glared at the CD player as if *it* were at fault for Cameron not responding. "You're a piece of work, I *know* you heard me." Patricia Storm punched the Off button with her thumb.

"Maaa," groaned Cameron, "that's the coolest song ever!"

"And you're gonna be in the tenth grade *forever* if you don't get going right now. It's already past eight."

"I got cramps. Can I stay home?"

"It's called No."

"But my stomach really hurts."

"Your period was over last week. No."

"Maaa . . ."

"Don't *maaa* me to death." She looked from the brush in her daughter's hand to the hair on her head. "And you need to drag your . . . mic . . . through that . . ."—she searched for the right words—"mound of tumbleweed. For the life of me, pretty as you are, I don't know why you won't get it permed—"

"Maaa . . ." interrupted Cameron, cutting short the sentence. But she still heard her mother's usual words in her head anyway—*like a civilized girl.*

Her mother was gone as abruptly as she'd appeared. Sounds traveled through the thin walls of the one-bedroom house as if through open windows. Cameron sat on her bed, listening. There was the dry, rhythmic sound of hair being brushed, hair her mother wore in a smooth ponytail held at the neck by a silver clip. The scrape of metal chair legs as she sat down at the thrift-store vanity table to paint her lips red and highlight her blue eyes with blue mascara. Cameron's

4

own blue eyes, said her mother, came from Norwegian grand-parents, and her olive skin from the Italian dad she'd never known. Hangers slid and clinked against each other on the metal clothes rack used for a closet. Her mother was choosing a jacket light enough for the springtime weather. Probably the pink and purple one she liked so much, with the white patent leather belt that Cameron hated.

Soon she was at the front door shouting a slew of instructions for her daughter to follow.

"Make sure you eat something, you can't learn on an empty stomach! Take the hamburger meat out of the freezer if you still want chili for dinner! Don't forget to lock *all* the locks, the new people down the block don't look too kosher! And by the way, that shirt you got on smells a little ripe! Have a good day at school, hon, and get going, it's twenty after!"

The only bedroom in the house was Cameron's. Her mother insisted on sleeping in what was actually a storage space. Cameron had decorated her room with care. Wall posters celebrated rock groups and boy bands. Teen magazine pictures taped on the mirror frame formed a celebrity halo around her reflection. Britney Spears in a sequined bustier with a glittery thong peeking over low-slung hip-huggers. Gwen Stefani pasty in heavy makeup and gangsta-girl baggies. Mariah Carey oozing out of a doll-size pink minidress. Hilary Duff sporting a skull on her metal belt and a "You're So Yesterday" black T-shirt. And top and center like the crowning ornament on a Christmas tree, a punked-out Avril Lavigne with electric guitar, wristbands, sideways cap, sleeveless men's undershirt, and black tie.

Cameron contemplated her hair in the mirror, brushed the sides down, and pushed it all under an FDNY baseball cap. She raised her arm and sniffed her T-shirt. Maybe she *had* worn it one day too many, she wasn't sure. She sniffed it again. Whatever. Nobody would be getting close enough to notice anyway. She turned the CD player back on, imitated Avril's signature move—throwing up horns—then brought her three upraised fingers down to an imaginary guitar. With her mother gone, she was no longer limited to mouthing the words, she could sing out loud. And she did, belting out lyrics about confusion and craziness as though she herself had written them. No way was she rushing off to school. Only nerds arrived on time for homeroom roll call.

"Cameron, may I speak to you a moment?" asked Miss Levin with a polite chill in her voice.

"Me?" Cameron had slipped into the classroom through the back door, eased out of her Army surplus jacket, and slithered into the seat next to her friend Amanda.

"No, not you—Minnie Mouse. Is there another Cameron in the class?"

Cameron went to the front of the classroom, passing rows of chair desks and snickering students.

At the desk she looked at Miss Paula Levin's shapely red lips, long mascaraed lashes, and slicked-back hair. She remembered how excited her mom had been at their first parent-teacher meeting. Not about Cameron's grades, which were below average. What her mother couldn't get over was how much Miss Levin looked like a young version of some singer named Carly Simon.

"You're late. Again."

"I'm really sorry, Miss Levin. I totally ran for the bus which was only a few feet—*inches*, come to think of it—from the bus stop, and I was pounding on the side of the bus like a maniac but the driver was *sooo* not opening the doors. It's really his fault that I'm late."

Miss Levin was writing the whole time Cameron was talking and didn't once look up.

"Yesterday it was the rain's fault and the day before it was your ailing mother's fault and the day before that it was God's fault for making you a girl who gets monthly cramps. Take this to Mr. Siciliano at the end of the period. We'll let him figure out who's at fault."

Giggling spread through the room. Cameron took the guidance counselor referral form and returned to her seat. She used to get bugged when kids laughed at her but now she didn't care. That's just what people do: laugh when someone else gets in trouble because they're so glad it's not them. She had grown up with most of them, except for the Russians and the Pakistanis, who were new to the Midwood neighborhood, and a few black kids from some housing project somewhere. Some were nerdy, some were total pains, but most of them were pretty okay. And then there were the way cool ones like Amanda. Amanda was the most fun of her friends and also *numero uno* in their class, which could've made her a nerd if not for her being fun. She wanted to be a vet when she grew up. P, who was the greatest dancer, already knew she was going to nursing school. Crazy Crystal, with her squealy voice, swore she'd be some kind of famous something, she just didn't know what. Cameron had no future plans either, so at least she and Crystal were in the same sinking boat.

"Off to see the Godson again, huh?" teased Amanda, as Cameron took her seat. "You know, Cam, you're on your way to becoming a real mafia moll with these daily visits. I bet you're late on purpose just so you—"

"Amanda!" yelled the teacher, giving Amanda her famous stern glare. Cameron giggled behind her hand.

At the sound of the bell the class burst into a commotion of scraping chairs and noisy conversation. Cameron set out for her disciplinary meeting. Amanda promised to save her a seat in world history class. Kids greeted Cameron in the hallway. "Hey, Cam, what's up!" "Yo, Camelhump!" "Cam, where're you going, class is *this* way!"

A student was in with Mr. Siciliano, so she pulled her cell phone from her bag and started playing solitaire. After what seemed like forever, the door opened and out came a scowling boy, followed by the counselor.

"Well, look who's back," said Mr. Siciliano. "Haven't seen you in about . . . twenty-four hours."

As the name suggested, Malcolm Siciliano was only half Italian. But that was enough to fuel the students' mafia jokes and earn him the "Godson" nickname.

"Come in, Miss Storm." He shook her hand.

Mr. Siciliano addressed all the students as Mister and Miss. He was the only faculty member who dressed in business suits, starched shirts, and elegant ties. Cameron sat down and repeated her tale about the runaway bus, not a word of it true.

"So what you're saying is that the bus driver refused to open the door, gave you the finger, and deliberately drove away? Frankly, Miss Storm, your story wouldn't persuade even the most gullible of guidance counselors. If we're going to work together you have to be honest with me."

He turned his swivel chair to the desk, opened a file, and began reading.

"Let's see, you're fifteen years old and in the process of digging yourself into a pretty deep hole. Your record is not stellar, my friend. You're often late, you're failing geometry, and you're barely passing language arts."

"And?" She yawned.

"*And* . . . your best grades are in world history, but the teacher notes that she suspects copying."

"Whoa! How could Miss Gallstones—"

"*Goldstone*. Miss *Goldstone*."

"—say that?! Omigod, that is so not right of her, she totally hated me from Day One. She's evil."

"Don't be silly. The teachers don't hate any of our students. It says here that you ace the exam each time you happen to be sitting near Amanda Vine, but otherwise . . ."

"Pure evil."

She sat in silence, biting her nails. Why *shouldn't* Amanda help her? That's what friends were for.

The counselor placed his glasses on top of the file and swiveled back around. "Enough negativity. You're reading at your grade level and I know you can do the work. Are there other issues? How're things going in general—friendships, family—everything okay?"

No, there were no issues. She had three best friends, and she and her mom got on pretty good except for hassles over certain things like clothes and chores and hair.

Friends were important, he said, and every generation thinks it has the best music. He also hated doing chores and to his eye, her hair was fine.

Whatever. Cameron opened her mouth wide and let out a long, fake yawn. "Can I go now? I'm missing class." She licked the blood from her bitten cuticle.

He made her promise to be more punctual and work on raising her grades. They shook hands and she rushed out.

She stood alone in the empty corridor, checked the time on her cell phone. Class was almost half over. She'd seem like a total moron showing up midway. Besides, she was in no mood to see evil Miss Gallstones. She sent Crystal a text message.

"Want 2go AWOL?"

The school had a rule that cell phones had to be turned off in class but everybody just put them on Vibrate and sent text messages back and forth. She hoped Crystal would be able to slip her an answer. After a few minutes, the phone trembled in her palm. Yes! She could always count on Crystal.

"NW."

No way? What kind of answer was that?

"EM?" replied Cameron. She wanted to say a lot more than *excuse me?* but hoped she could convince her friend to hang out, go to the mall or the beach. Crystal's response dashed that hope.

"N class. CUL."

Since when did being in class stop Crystal from slipping out a back door? And what was with the *see you later* blow-off? Cameron's fingers pounded away.

"YG2BKM. PU. CMON. PLS."

She reread her message. *You've got to be kidding me. That stinks.* The *come on, please* part sounded pretty pathetic, but she pressed Send anyway and waited near the exit for an answer. Finally, the phone quivered.

"SRY. G2G. LYLAS."

Sorry. Got to go. Love you like a sis. That was it? Whatever. She typed in a message to P, who was cooler than Crystal anyway and would most definitely come through for her.

"P, U there? TMB ASAP."

She waited.

"Prudence, TMB!"

She'd *said* "text me back" but the phone lay dead in her hand. P probably didn't even have hers on, which was so lame of her. Bummer, that really sucked. She flipped shut her phone and shoved open the exit door.

two

Outside, the air smelled of car exhaust and flower buds, the school being located next to a main avenue and not far from a botanical garden. Cameron was headed no place in particular. It just felt good to move and breathe in open spaces. Winter had been cold and sulky and she'd spent most of her time inside. The spring sun was hot and popcorn clouds sat high in the bright sky. The frayed hems of her loose jeans swept the pavement as she walked. She pulled off her cap and stuck it in her knapsack. As she draped her jacket over her shoulder a sour smell wafted from her armpit. She frowned, regretting not taking her mom's advice about changing the T-shirt. There was just something about advice from her mom that made her want to do the opposite. On general principle. Even when she knew her mom was right.

She wasn't very far from her own block, but the houses she passed seemed to belong to a different neighborhood.

Brooklyn was like that though, from one block to another the whole world could change. These houses weren't hooked together, like where she lived, but stood alone and grand behind brick walls. And they were massive, two and three stories tall, with arched entryways and manicured shrubbery going all the way around. Whenever she walked by them she looked for the residents, curious as to who lived that way. But she never saw anyone go in or out. Her mom said the owners were rich dealers of diamonds and furs, and that if Cameron studied hard and got a good job they'd integrate the block. Right. As cleaning ladies.

A Hummer slowed into pace with her steps.

"*Mira, mami!* You lookin' good from the back, you need a ride?"

A blast of horns and shouts erupted before she could stick out her tongue and flip them off.

They shouted "stuck-up *blanca!*" as they drove off.

"Jerks!" she yelled back.

She followed Ocean Avenue all the way to the ocean, where she took off her sneakers and socks and jammed them, along with her jacket, into her knapsack. She stepped barefoot onto the beach, picked up a handful of rocks, and threw one after the other as far as they could fly, watching them vanish with a small splash.

People dotted the beach from one end to the other, some dodging the sun under umbrellas, others baking their oil-slicked bodies on towels. As she walked her toes sank deep into the warm sand. Sagging, sunburned old men on beach chairs checked her out from behind sunglasses. Teenagers who also should've been in school lay stretched out on jackets, sat in circles, chased each other, screaming, into the nippy ocean.

A mom and dad in matching purple swimwear dipped a little girl over and over in the shallow surf, the kid squealing as the water lapped her stubby legs. Cameron watched from a short distance, imagining herself as the girl, except for the dad part. That topic had been so off-limits for so long that she rarely wondered about her father, other than on Father's Day. The couple noticed her. Taking his daughter's little wrists in his hands, the father waved her fat arms.

"See the girl?" he cooed. "Wave to the nice girl."

Cameron waved back and walked on. The sun glared directly above her head and her legs had gained a hundred pounds each. She dropped first the knapsack then herself onto the glinting sand. The smell of amusement park food made her stomach growl. A hot dog and French fries from Nathan's sounded really good, but she had no money. A light wind rode in on the waves and tousled her hair. The water was a dingy bluish color. Her mind shaped thoughts into vivid daydreams. Of Jet-Skiing out to the horizon. Surfing a wall of wave in a perfectly balanced crouch. Swimming for miles, escorted by dolphins. She'd never Jet-Skied or surfed and immediately sank in swimming pools, but none of that spoiled her pleasurable reverie.

A man plopped down a few feet away, but still way too close for a stranger. "This seat taken?" he said. His flat, black hair hung down to his shoulders and looked deliberately greasy, like he put pomade in it. He had small eyes and a large nose, and his rolled-up pants exposed stubby hair on his crunched-up toes and thick ankles.

"Sure is pretty, am I right? But Brooklyn water's nothing compared to what they got over there in Hawaii. You been? Yeah, that water's blue as a pretty blonde's blue eyes—or a brunette's." He made a weird snorting sound. "I'm digging your shirt . . . 'Enter at Your Own Risk,' huh?" He laughed a creepy laugh. "Nothing ventured nothing gained, am I right? The name's Napoleon by the way, but the kids call me Neon, like the lights. And you?"

Cameron stared into the distance. But ignoring him wasn't shutting this guy up one bit, he kept talking as if they were having a conversation.

"No school today or playing hooky? Hey, you won't get no flak from me, I hated the books too. I was into the music thing, you know, cutting out to go jam for hours in somebody's basement, yeah. You look like you dig music too. You thirsty?"

Two cans of beer appeared. The man squished one down in the sand next to her, opened the other and took a noisy slurp. She thought about getting up but figured what could he do in front of all those people? Anyway, she was there first.

So she continued to look straight ahead, her eyes focused on the line joining the ocean to the sky.

"Not a Chatty Cathy, huh? Hey, I'm solid with silence too, yeah, the whole *being within* thing, we're talking *connection*, that's what I seek, what you seek, what we all seek, and I'm talking animals, trees, people . . . Nothing wants to be lonely, am I right?"

A twinge of longing shot through her and for a second she almost responded. But she caught herself. Don't talk to strangers. Especially strange ones. If only Crystal and P hadn't ditzed out on her, she wouldn't be stuck with this mutant.

"So I was mentioning music 'cause I seen you way down the beach all alone skipping rocks—you got a good arm—and I'm thinking, that girl's perfect for the band—the funky threads, the wild hair, the nice shape. See, I'm putting together a punk-rock group of girls about your age, fourteen, fifteen. I don't got a name yet but I'm thinking something like Ruff Lolitas or the Riotgirl Dolls."

He leaned back on one elbow, still conversing with Cameron's side.

"Interested? 'Cause if so"—he began drawing in the sand with his finger—"I give you something, you give me something . . ."

That was it. Cameron leapt to her feet, knapsack in hand.

"Sure, dude, why don't I give it to you right now? How about a nice SANDwich!"

Like a soccer star, she swung her foot just so, shooting a storm of sand into the man's face and hair. His coughs and curses grew fainter as she ran, her heart pounding, her hands trembling. It wasn't that she was scared, it was more a feeling of war, like everything was a battle. With her mom, the teachers, the counselor, the Hummer boys, and now this total deviant who was surely listed on some perv registry.

She followed the boardwalk, catching her breath. Gamestand hucksters called to her, "Step right up, miss, try your luck! For a dollar a play, might be your lucky day!" At the candied-apples stand she pondered what to do next when a dark-skinned woman wearing an ankle-length black skirt handed her a pamphlet entitled "What Would Jesus Do?"

"You all right? Your face all red, you need some water? Look at you, cute as a button and hanging around out here by yourself, lost."

"I'm okay, thanks. And I'm not lost. I'm at Coney Island."

"Oh, honey, lost is wrote all over you like those hypoglyppics they got in them caves. Lost but not alone, because your best friend is by your side. Have you met your best friend? His name is Jesus Christ and He will guide your every move if you take Him in your heart as your . . ."

Cameron didn't know what she believed in, if anything, but she wasn't about to be converted at an amusement park.

"Thanks, but I'm Jewish," she lied, easing away.

"Child, Jesus was Jewish too." The woman reached into

her oversize pocketbook and pulled out another pamphlet. "Have you heard of Jews for Jesus?"

Once Cameron had put a safe distance between herself and the evangelist, she stopped to think. It was lunchtime. She'd missed world history and earth science, and kids were already scarfing down whatever gross lunch was being served in the cafeteria. She could grab something at the house and eat on her way back to school or "happen by" her mom's salon, which was closer. What *would* Jesus do? *Most definitely* go for the free food with His mom.

Madame Elga's Nails-Only Luxury Salon could have used a fresh coat of polish on its flaking pink door. Like the owner, it had seen better days. Elga Oblomovna had been a slender mail-order bride when she arrived on Brooklyn's shores to meet her future husband. The timing of the marriage couldn't have been worse, falling as it did in the middle of a Brighton Beach mob war. Raining down with the celebratory rice fell a hail of bullets that left the bride a weeping widow. That very evening she found a suitcase of hundred-dollar bills, which she used to buy a nail-technician diploma on the black market and lease space for a salon.

In the early days, the bustling salon catered to a monied clientele from nearby Oceanview Condos, but as organized crime convictions sent husbands up the river, the fingernails of their nouveau-broke wives went to ruin. Three decades later, thickened by time and Russian sausages, an embittered and pudgy Elga Oblomovna ran her business lackadaisically.

The *bing-bong* of the salon's front door ended the woman's daily afternoon nap.

"Irina!" she cried excitedly from her office. "Is that my dear Olga Petrova arriving?"

She referred to all her clients as *my dear*, at least when they were within earshot. Warmth, she'd declared, was good for business. She kept for herself the salon's few remaining wealthy clients, like that chronic no-show Olga Petrova who was already an hour late.

"No, madame," answered Irina, "it is Trisha's girl!"

"Dammit!" snarled the boss, giving her office door a violent kick.

Cameron heard a loud slam as she stepped into the salon. What sounded like some kind of ballet music was playing in the background. Most of the dozen or so tables stood empty except for some bottles of gaudy polish. She liked the women who worked with her mother. They wore white smocks with their names stitched in red over the breast pocket and were nice. She surveyed the room in search of her mom. There was Valya, who didn't look much older than Cameron herself, chatting with an orange-haired woman. The young Ukrainian smiled and winked at Cameron, then resumed her work. Aging, nearsighted Ludmila was hunched over the hand of a redhead posed at the salon's huge picture window. Anna, a new hire with no clients of her own, sat with legs crossed, idly painting her own nails. She waved hello with her polish brush. Irina held up a gloved hand.

"Hi, Irina, I came to see my mom," said Cameron. Sometimes just seeing her mother stirred a surge of emotion.

"Cameroon! How is my dear lovely girl today? You been in sun, I see, skin always so nice and tan." She took Cameron's hand and examined it. "You doing something with those nails? Oh, look how terrible, so short and chewy! Why you don't let Irina give you nice nail wrap with a shimmery red polish?"

Every time she visited the salon one of the women would propose artificial nails or want to paint her real ones some orangey red color.

"Maybe for my high school graduation I'll try it, but not today."

"If anyone's beautifying her nails when she graduates," said Patricia, walking over, "it's gonna be her mom." She kissed Cameron's cheek, whispering, "Welcome to the Gulag." She'd just finished up with a client and peeled off her protective gloves. "Did you make it to school on time? And lock all three locks? You already had lunch? Your pants are caked with sand, you went to the beach?" She inhaled. "Hmmph, you didn't change your shirt."

The warm buzz Cameron had felt upon seeing her mother disappeared. Why did she always have to ask a bunch of questions at once?

"Yep. Yep. Nope. Yep."

"Hey, you, don't yep and nope me to death." Cameron's windblown hair drew her attention. "Thought you were gonna do something with that mane." She gave her daughter a playful pinch. "Come on over to the table and behold a nail technology expert at work. Soon as I'm done with my next client we'll eat. You sure you're gonna have enough time? When's your next class?"

A stout woman with bleached yellowish hair and gobs of eye makeup was waiting. Polish bottles of pinkish red and dark red, burgundy and purple, mauve and neutral covered the nail table.

"Svetlana, have you met my daughter?"

"No, not before," said the woman, raising her eyebrows. "Not blond like mother? Blond is important in America, even the blacks are blondes. Her dark hair from father?"

Patricia quickly asked the client if she'd removed her old polish and washed her hands, then said to Cameron, "Svetlana's one of my favorite clients, straight from Moscow. Have you studied anything about Moscow in school?"

"Yeah, it's freezing cold there." A favorite client? Cameron had heard about Svetlana, a "friggin' piece of work," who took forever to choose a polish color, then would want her nails re-polished a million and one times because she didn't like the color.

Patricia applied polish to disks and presented the color wheels to Svetlana.

"So what will it be today?" She contracted her mouth into a smile.

Svetlana peered, mumbled to herself, and peered some more.

"Hmmm, not so sure today. Don't show me the brown wheel, I'm too fair for the brownish beige kind of colors. I am thinking Calypso Punch or Sonora Sunset, don't know."

Patricia gave Cameron a "see what I mean" look, then donned her smile.

"Maybe I go with simple French manicure. I am thinking off-white with pink opal over it, you think?"

The decision was made, but as soon as the pearlized white polish was applied to her nails, Svetlana began critiquing everything and pulling her hand away to check the work. Cameron burst out laughing when her mother snatched the woman's hand back.

"I can't see your nails if you can, and if I don't see them, they don't get polished correctly. Now for chrissakes, let me do my friggin' job . . . my dear Svetlana."

three

A crush of people packed into Nathan's Famous restaurant. Cameron's mother kept checking her watch. "I don't know why I let you talk me into coming all the way out here to oombatzland when there's a sandwich shop next door to my work."

"What . . . is *oombatzland*?"

"Oombatzland," answered Patricia, "is any place that takes me the hell out of my way. Like right here. We're gonna have all of three minutes to eat."

Mentally, Cameron was already eating—swallowing simply thinking of the hot dog with everything on it she'd be munching in a few minutes. The food at Nathan's was worlds cooler than some boring sandwich. Should she have a medium or large French fries? she pondered. Large. With a jumbo orange drink. She figured that on such a nice day all the outside tables were probably taken, but she was confident they'd find a space to squeeze in at the counter.

"Next customer!" The checkout girl's bark startled her to attention and she gave their order.

"Scuse us, scuse us," insisted Patricia, carving a path for them.

Cameron followed her mother, balancing the food on a bright orange tray. From the corner of her eye she spied a paunchy, balding man at the very end of the counter wiping his mouth, about to leave. She pounced.

"Can we fit in here?" Without waiting for an answer she set their tray down, nudging his tray to the side.

"Not"—he ran his eyes over them both—"a problem, babydolls, I was just leaving. Always glad to assist a pair of babes in distress."

He burped and strolled away in cracked sandals and faded green-plaid shorts.

"Well, ain't *that* a sight to cut a babe's appetite," snickered Patricia.

"Truly." Even though the guy was gross, Cameron felt kind of proud that he called her mom a "babe." She *was* pretty nice-looking for her age.

Between mouthfuls, they spoke in loud voices to compete with the carousel's bouncy organ, the roller coaster's clanking roar, and a constant cheery jingle that seemed to emanate from the air itself. Patricia vented about her tightwad lunatic of a boss, who'd tried in vain to make them parade around wearing sandwich boards to attract clients. They all knew Elga had money up the wazoo and was playing poor so as not to pay them what they deserved. It was going on four years she'd been working there and the only raise she ever saw was that pain-in-the-A Svetlana's raised eyebrow.

Cameron couldn't stop laughing. When her mom got going, she was hilarious. If only she would stay that way, and not get into cranky moods about stuff that wasn't even important. Like the bottoms of dragging jeans that leave a little dirt and a few twigs in the house. And dishes that are rinsed out instead of washed. And low grades in boring subjects you don't need to know for life anyway, like the periodic table of elements. Money was a constant problem, but Cameron knew there was little she could do to help. Maybe drop out and work in a place that hired dropouts, like a fast-food. Or a nail salon. Right. No way would her mom go for that.

Patricia drained the last drops of her diet soda. "So, hon, I know you didn't stop by the salon for a free frank and some fries. Are you okay? You seem *off* somehow. And don't tell me another one of your stories about a class trip to the beach, there's not a classmate of yours in sight. Your mother wasn't born yesterday, you know. I'm not gonna stand for you cutting school, you *know* that."

"*Okay*. I went to the beach. By myself. But I *had* to get some air because Miss Gallstones thinks she's some kind of evil genius but she's just evil without the genius and she told the guidance counselor I cheated on a test, which I *so* did not, and you know my friend Crystal? Well she totally blew me off, which I don't know *what* that's about but *whatever*, and P wouldn't answer her phone and the homeroom teacher called me Minnie Mouse in front of everybody—"

"Wait a sec, slow down! Who is Miss Gallstones and why would she accuse you of—"

"—and this freaky old dude tried to pick me up but I kicked sand in his face."

That last alarming tidbit erased from Patricia's mind everything that had come before.

"What man?" she exclaimed, taking hold of Cameron's wrist. "Did he hurt you? What'd I tell you about talking to strange men, Cameron? There's a world of sickos out here."

"Ma, I *didn't* talk to him. I didn't say a word. I kicked a huge mound of sand right in his ugly face. He couldn't do anything to me anyhow, on a beach full of people ready to jump in. Really, he was harmless."

"Harmless? You *hope*. You can't take those kinds of chances, Cameron. And how do you know anyone would've helped you? You can't rely on strangers, everyone looks out for number one."

"There was this mom and dad with a kid not that far from me and I know they would've come to the rescue because me and their daughter bonded."

"Cameron, you're too trusting. Your innocence is giving me agita."

"Sorry, Mom, I'll be more careful. It's just that I was already there, then this mutant comes over and sits—"

"Please." She kissed Cameron on the forehead. "You're all I got." A glance at her watch flipped her mood. "Holy shi . . . sheep, I gotta go! It's a quarter to. How're you gonna get back to school in time? Let's get you a cab . . . TAXI!!!! . . . Here, take this money, it shouldn't cost more than three or four bucks. And go straight home after school! And don't forget the meat from the freezer. I should be there at least by five thirty!"

A taxicab pulled up and Cameron climbed in. "Herbert Hoover High School, please."

From the back window she watched her mother hurrying down the block. A smile settled on her lips and she mouthed *Love you, Mom*. The festive Coney Island landscape whirled by—the merry-go-round, the Eldorado Bumper Cars, Steeplechase, the aquarium. Cameron loved the place, and indeed that whole section of Brooklyn. She'd be happy to spend her whole life there. Suddenly, her lap quivered. She rummaged through her knapsack. A message from P. "Hey QT, W/B." *Hey cutie, write back.* She was on her way, replied Cameron, and would be to class in no time.

P was doing a visual scan of the classroom when out of nowhere Cameron was suddenly in the seat next to her. The two friends hugged like they hadn't seen each other just the day before.

"Hey, sweets! Where'd you come from and why'd you call me Prudence in your message, schmo face? You know I hate that name." P disliked her last name, Darling, even more than her first, but it suited her perfectly because she was the darling of all the boys.

"That's what you get for not answering my message."

"Whatever. My phone wasn't on. You're gonna get something worse if you call me Prudence again."

Prudence Darling was the crush of many, having the high cheekbones, straight nose, and blond locks of a Ralph Lauren model. And her rugged Brooklyn longshoreman accent added a fearsome, exciting quality. But the Ralph Lauren connection ended with her wardrobe—faded tops, wrinkled genie pants, and scuffed construction boots.

"You won't believe my day, P, it's been the pits."

She recounted the "beach freak" story. P loved the part about the *sand*wich and said if that had happened to her, she would've stomped his face in. Cameron nodded toward the teacher. "What letter is he up to? Did he call me already?"

She was in luck. Mr. Robinson hadn't yet made it to "S."

"Sufi Pundari? Excellent! Tobias Richland? Please raise your hand if you're present! Tobias Richland! Thank you, Toby."

Langston Robinson was handsome like the black actors on TV cop shows. Tall and abundantly muscled, he always wore matching turtlenecks and slacks, usually black. When she and P Googled him, along with all their teachers and most everyone they met, they found out that the once aspiring actor had been an extra on a black sitcom and had even done television commercials. For that, he was given the L Word Award—Loser—for becoming a high school teacher instead of a rich movie star.

"Sabeth Roth? You here! What, the mall's closed today? Jeanne Rural? Jeanne! There you are, what a nice surprise!"

The failed actor intoned each name as if a simple roll call were one of the dramatic arts.

"Frances Shelley? Paging Frances Shelley! Welcome back, stranger! Cameron Storm?"

Cameron waved from the back row. "Here!"

". . . Taylor Teng? Shanelle Williams? . . ."

Marty Zuckerman was marked absent and living-arts class began. Mr. Robinson wrote across the board in dramatic block letters OTHELLO—THE THEATRE OF WILLIAM SHAKE-SPEARE, setting off a chorus of groans and complaints.

He'd assigned *Othello* the week before and the class was supposed to discuss it.

"I didn't understand a thing," confessed one student.

"Me neither," added another. "That story wasn't even wrote in good English from the giddyup."

A girl whispered to another, "Who spells theater with an 're'? That is *sooo* gay."

A boy loudly observed, "Shakespeare sucks!"

The teacher raised his hands. "Yes, yes, I know. You'd all rather be trampled by elephants than study one of the great pieces of writing by the English-speaking world's greatest dramatist. What plays, pray tell, do *you* all like?"

"PlayStation!" shouted Cameron, her voice disguised in a low rasp.

Mr. Robinson pursed his lips in annoyance, scrutinizing the students' faces in search of the culprit comedian. "Very funny, whoever said that."

For those who hadn't read the play, he summarized its plot in terms he hoped would intrigue the class.

"*Othello* was written in 1604 but the story is rich with contemporary issues, if you'll just permit yourselves to embrace the old English."

"*Love* me some Olde English, especially straight out the bottle!" yelled P.

Mr. Robinson gave a loud clap of his hands to show he would tolerate no more interruptions.

"Silence! It is an eminently human tale about race, gender, and sex."

This last word drew titters from all over the classroom.

"The thumbnail sketch for you slackers who may not have done the reading assignment is this: a successful black man living in a white world succumbs to jealousy and murders his wife." He had their attention. "Think O. J. Simpson."

"O.J. was framed!" shouted a boy.

"Not! He's guilty as Michael Jackson!" yelled a girl.

"Michael's innocent!" challenged another. "He got off, right?!"

"He got *away*," declared someone else.

Another loud clap ended the debate.

"Calm down people, forget O.J. and Michael. Our concern is with the noble Moor of Venice, who throughout the play is described in racially charged language like 'thicklips,' 'sooty,' and 'an old black ram.' This has led some critics to consider *Othello* to be strictly about race. Anyone have an opinion about that? Toby . . . no? Frances . . . unprepared again? Cameron?"

Othello was very long and Cameron only read long stories if they were crammed with unicorns, goblins, and werewolves or were about teenage girls bugging out. But she *had* read the slacker summary of the play.

"It seemed to me like they all had race issues. I felt sorry for Othello because he was all tripped out about being a Moor, you know, black, and that's how Iago was able to make him believe his wife was cheating with a white guy."

"Good analysis, Cameron. Do you all agree that the story is essentially racial or could there be something else going on here?"

A girl wearing matching eyebrow rings raised her chubby hand.

"I think it's more about, like, being different. Okay, so he happened to be an African dude in an Italian world, but think about it, Othello coulda been anything—handicapped, gay, a person of size—"

"Just say *fat*!"

The minority of kids who weren't overweight laughed wildly.

"Silence!" warned the teacher.

"—and people woulda treated him the same way—bad."

"Interesting . . . interesting," said Mr. Robinson. "Responses? Comments? Reactions to Fanny's point of view?"

"Yeah," offered Jeanne, "they didn't have handicapped people back then!"

"Yes, they so *did*," retorted Fanny. "What do you think the Hunchback of Notre Dame was?"

P shot her hand up and didn't wait to be called on.

"Not for nothing, but you guys are missing the whole point. That nut job smothered his wife to death, and she was innocent! Then he's like, poor me, I was crazy in love or however he put it . . . I don't remember his exact words."

Mr. Robinson did, as he had *been* Othello in a college production his senior year.

" 'Then must you speak of One that lov'd not wisely but too well,' " he recited in his best Shakespearean accent. A few smirking sounds were made, but he ignored them.

"Who remembers at what point Othello utters those famous words? Sabeth? Sabeth's biting her nails, so that must mean no. Taylor? Anyone?"

"I do," answered P. "It was right before he stabbed himself, which is exactly what O.J. should've done."

"I *told* y'all my man O.J. was set up!"

"That's right," agreed Shanelle, "and just like O.J.'s trial,

Othello's situation was so about SWB—Succeeding While Black. All the whites were racist in those days. One of the footnotes said the Queen had already passed a law in 1601 banishing 'negars'—n-e-g-a-r-s—from England. She was steady hatin' on us and couldn't even *spell* the word."

Sandy-haired Tobias Richland raised his hand and stood up. The spoiled son of a successful plastic surgeon, he dressed in gangsta baggies and T-shirts celebrating dead rappers.

"I feel you, Shanelle, but listen up. I'm white, ah-ight, but me and Othello would've been tight homeys back in the day, 'cause I'm so like totally about one love and that punk Iago wasn't nuthin' but a hater, you feel me?"

No, she did *not*, Shanelle said, calling Toby an Eminem wannabe and Eminem a black wannabe. She didn't mince words. "So just sit your pimply tail down, Toby, because we all know you would've been tight all right . . . with the Queen."

It took Mr. Robinson a good five minutes to calm down the hysterical class. Then they had a spirited debate about self-esteem, race, and interracial dating. Cameron and P held their own private discussion.

"What about you, P, would you have a boyfriend from a different race?"

P shifted her eyes back and forth as though eavesdroppers might be near.

"Been there, done that," she said.

"Lie! Stop goofing around."

"I'm not, Cam. I been there and I did that. You know who

Jerome Davis is, right, the black guy on the fencing team?"

"Yeah, but he's a *senior*! Are you lying? You're totally lying. If you did, how come none of us knew?" Cameron was skeptical. The only guys she ever saw P with were WASPs like *her*.

"Us *who*?"

"*Us* your best friends, *hellooo*, me, Amanda, and Crystal."

P shook her head sassily. "I had to swear to keep it on the d-low, super secret. He said if it got out, the blacks would put him down and the whites would beat him up. It was *ages* ago anyway and only lasted maybe a month, no, three weeks. Not for nothing but it's still a secret, so don't go blabbing to *anyone* . . . I'm only telling *you*."

"Whoa . . . I still can't believe you never said anything." She pulled at her curls. "Sooo?"

"So *what*?"

"You know . . . sooo?"

P leaned close to Cameron's ear. "Well, Cam, you know what they say: Once you go black, you can never go back."

Cameron pinched her nose and pressed her lips together not to burst out laughing.

P leaned in closer. "And there's another part: If you stay white, you'll always be right."

They covered their mouths, chuckling. P asked Cameron the same question.

"Cough up to it, Cam. You know you would too."

"I don't know. I'm not prejudiced or anything, but being

white, it's just easier to go out with a white guy, you know, it's more like . . . normal. But I guess if you fall in love like you and Jerome and can't help it . . ."

"We weren't in love," said P with a sly grin, "we were in lust."

They were still giggling and whispering when someone seated behind them passed Cameron a note. It was Tobias. Inside a fat heart he'd written "Toby and Cam, destined 2B 2gether." They'd gone to the movies twice, sat together at lunch three times, made out in the gym once, and then it was finished. He was too lame, with his weird blended dialect of dudespeak and Ebonics. Months later, he still liked her but she couldn't have been more over it.

She held open the love note so P could read it too, wrote under the heart "4never," crumpled it into a ball, and tossed it over her shoulder, striking Toby on the nose.

P twisted around to face him. "Stop stalking, keep walking. Do it and like it."

He held up his fingers in a peace sign, placed two on his lips, and blew Cameron a kiss. P and Cameron went "ewww," gave each other high fives, played several games of hangman, then text-messaged Amanda and Crystal to meet them at the mall after school.

four

The vast and dilapidated Kings Plaza shopping mall was lined with overpriced stores armed with anti-shoplifting hidden cameras. It was quite far from any subway and dangerously close to a seedy bus terminal plastered with missing-persons posters. No mother wanted her daughter dawdling in such a place, but few could stop them. Resembling more an eighteen-year-old woman than the fifteen-year-old girl she was, Amanda lingered outside Victoria's Secret in a white cashmere V-neck sweater, dark magenta capris, and off-white Mary Jane–style sneakers. She pretended not to notice the ogling boys and leering men as she brushed her hair in the store window reflection. A chorus of sudden cries made some nearby shoppers jump.

"Amaaanda!"

Cameron and P had arrived. The girls ran screaming toward each other with outstretched arms, as if they had been separated for *ages.*

"Caaam! *P!*"

Wrapped in a ball of hugs the high schoolers hopped up and down, squealing.

"*Omigod!*" shrieked Amanda, glimpsing Crystal in the distance.

"Cry*staaal!*" roared the trinity.

A slight girl bounded over, wearing red cowboy boots adorned with Happy Bunny stickers, a polka-dot shirt, and a short plaid skirt. The ecstatic trio became a hysterical quartet, with more hops and squeals. Amanda playfully scolded Cameron for not showing up for world history class that morning after she'd gone to the trouble, thankyouverymuch, of saving a seat. P said not for nothing but Cameron had learned much more from some Coney Island Beach nut job. Cameron repeated the story to Amanda and Crystal.

"It's really Crystal's fault for blowing me off. If I hadn't been alone . . ."

"Um, you know," shrilled Crystal, "I don't think it's like right to blame me, I mean like, *hellooo*, who knew?"

It was always fun to mess with the high-strung baby of the group, who, having skipped a grade, was a sophomore even though only fourteen.

"You know you so should've been there," said Cameron in a blaming tone.

Crystal's mouth opened, her eyebrows jumped, and her head shook in fervent denial.

"No, but . . . you're not the boss of me, God is. And besides that's mega unfair because I was in class—"

"You're not the boss of me, you're not the boss of me . . . Why do you always say that?" taunted Cameron. "It's so . . . backwards."

"Cam, you're hurting me *sooo* much."

Cameron pushed out her lower lip. "And?"

Amanda caressed Crystal's face. "Awww, she hurt you? Come to mama."

Crystal laid her head on Amanda's shoulder.

"Oh, don't get your panties in a wad, Crystal, I'm only kidding. Why do you have to be so high all the time? High-pitched, high-strung, and high-maintenance? Truth is, P blew me off too, so it's as much her fault."

"Suck it up like a big girl, Camel lips," smirked P. *"Do* it and *like* it!"

The flush of emotion drained from Crystal's face and her good humor returned. They looped arms and bounced their way through the busy mall, window-shopping and boy-watching. In and out of stores they went, trying on skirts no wider than ribbons, squeezing their small breasts into smaller bustiers, and wobbling around on perilously high heels. Cameron, who was turning sixteen in the summer, tried on potential birthday outfits, everything from skater girl to punk chick to polished deb. Her three-judge fashion panel loudly approved or disapproved each look but mostly discussed what *they'd* be wearing to the party. Bopping past window displays, they sought out anything to do that might be fun. Crystal's idea to snatch one of the electronic wheelchairs for the handicapped and go for a joyride met with loud scorn. P was hungry and suggested going to the mall diner. Great idea, agreed the others, but who had money? Wealthy from raiding her father's gallon jars of quarters, she offered to lend—and she *meant* lend—them all snack money.

The pale waitress gave them a booth, which soon smelled of Reuben sandwiches and hamburgers, onion rings and fries and strong pickles. The conversation was limited to "hmmms" and "yumms" as they scarfed down their food. Two older teenagers with fake brown ponytails strutted by in numbingly tight jeans and bulging midriff tops that said "Project Grrrl." Their two-inch polka-dot fingernails looked both decorative and deadly. They disappeared into the restaurant. Crystal was quick to comment.

"Um, I don't really see how like that's something to be proud of, you know, as far as being from a project. It just means you're poor, black, on welfare, and wear booty-clothes."

Amanda sneered. "Why's your name even Crystal? Your brain is so *not* clear. Your mom should've called you Opaque. You can't say a whole group of people are all one thing, that's really dumb. Sure, people in the projects are probably poor, but a lot of them work and aren't on welfare. Anyway, everybody wants to be black these days, thankyouverymuch."

Crystal blinked her eyes and let her mouth drop open.

"Shut *up!* Get *out!* That's *craaazy!* *I* don't. Not that anything's wrong with it, it's just that, um . . ."

"That you're a nerdgirl," said Amanda. "What I should've said is everybody *cool* wants to be black. Eminem, Justin Timberlake, Gwen Stefani, Fergie from the Black-Eyed Peas. Look at Mariah Carey, she *is* black."

P took a noisy sip of Coke. "Black my ass."

"She's black, P. Cam, you remember the report I did on mixed-race celebrities?"

"Nope." Cameron was deep into her ketchupy onion rings.

"What do you mean *nope?* You were right there when I did my class presentation. Sage Brown, the teacher? Harvard? Cool? Black? Multicultures class, the one you're in? No bells ringing?"

Exasperation was getting the best of Amanda. "You really need to work on your *retention*, Cam. How're you going to get good grades if you have no memory? Ms. Sage Brown— smart, funny, relaxed, hot? Multicultures—diverse strengths, strength in diversity? Still no bells, huh?"

"Nope. I musta been out sick that day," said Cameron. She did remember, and Sage was her favorite teacher, but she was most definitely not going to let on now since Amanda was having such *attitude* with her ringing-bells thing.

Amanda tossed her hair. "Well *anyway*, Mariah Carey's father, Albert, was an African-American Venezuelan engineer."

Cameron twisted a curl around her finger. "A *what*? What the hell's an African-American Venezuelan?"

P blew bubbles in her soda. "It's a new nationality Amanda made up. Not for nothing, but I know for a fact that her mother's Irish, so that makes Mariah only half black. Anyway, she looks white as us and that's what it goes by." She blew more bubbles.

"No it *doesn't*, that's ridiculous *dahhh*," corrected Amanda. "It goes by your parents."

Cameron thought back to Othello. "You can't really say everybody wants to be black, Amanda. Today, in Mr. Robinson's class, we went over this play called *Othello*, where this black guy hates being black. But it's because of how people treat him. He wishes he were white so he doesn't have to deal with their prejudice."

"Puh-*leeze*, Cam," pleaded P, "don't bring up that wife-killing nut job. The only good thing about him is that he coughed up to the murder and offed himself too."

Amanda said Cameron was missing the point. All she was trying to say was that Mariah Carey is basically black. "Her voice is so Aretha! Who do you know that's white and can sing like that?"

Cameron said Joss Stone. P said Anastacia. Crystal said Celine Dion.

"Okay, guys," conceded Amanda, "I'll give you Anastacia,

she *does* have a big, gospel voice, and Joss too. But Celine Dion? Uh, *no*, Crystal. She sings great but she still sounds white."

Their waitress stopped at the table.

"Can I get you girls anything else?"

"Just the check," said P. The woman was about to move on to the next table when P stopped her. "Excuse me, miss? Is Mariah Carey white or black?"

"White," answered the waitress, "right?"

"Ha!" said P.

Crystal was munching on fries. "Amanda, you *really* think Eminem and all those people want to be black? Um, I don't *think* so. They only like to *act* black to be cool. Hey, let's be cool too and act black, like we're on that show *Girlfriends*."

"Yeah," said P, "it's all good."

Cam shook her head. "I *hate* when they say that . . . it's all good . . . I mean, what does that even like *mean*? Nothing can be *all* good, that is so whatever."

Crystal and P were on their feet with hands on hips, pushing their butts out and gyrating. Amanda dropped her head in her hands with an "Oh no." Cameron was cracking up.

"Oh no you *di'ent* put your hand in my face, girlfriend," squealed Crystal.

"Oh yes I *di-id*, homegirl," answered P.

"Then I'ma hafta *whack* you upside your head, playa hater," sneered Crystal.

"Yeah, well I looks too good to be knowin' y'all," sang P, "and I looks too good to be eatin' here . . . I'm conceited, I got a reason!"

Hard voices approached. It was the project girls and they were not amused.

"What's all that s'pose to be about?" seethed one girl, glaring at P, "y'all white girls dissin' us?"

The other girl moved within an inch of Crystal, who turned red, then white. Their noses almost touched.

"You one scrawny-looking mall rat, *girlfriend*."

Crystal cleared her throat. P stared. Amanda bit her lip. Cameron held her breath. This was not the time for one of Crystal's famously off-the-wall comments.

"What, you got something to say . . . cowgirl?"

"Uh . . . just that . . . um . . . you're not the boss of me."

As if they shared one pair of eyes, Cameron, Amanda, and P gaped at Crystal like they were seeing a car hurtle off a cliff.

The project girls exchanged *no-she-di'ent* looks.

"What you say, skank, you wanna take this outside?"

"Um . . . no, that's okay."

"I *thought* not, beeyatch." She tapped her friend's arm. "Come on, Asia, let's book before I hafta take some white-girl scalp up in here."

"Next time, blondie," hissed Asia, staring down P.

The two left with the same strut they walked in on.

"Not for nothing, but are you *crazy*, nut job, mouthing off to those project bimbos from hell?!" exclaimed P.

"Truly," agreed Cameron, "they most *definitely* would've kicked *all* our butts because of your big mouth."

"Crystal, Crystal, Crystal . . ." sighed Amanda, "*dahhh!*"

P quickly counted out her quarters and left them piled on the check. She hurried out, with Amanda and Cameron following closely. Behind them slunk Crystal, peering far ahead to make sure the project girls weren't waiting for her. The foursome walked to their neighborhood in sullen silence, broken now and again by jittery laughter.

Cameron turned the key in the lock and froze. She had forgotten to take the hamburger meat out to thaw! She pushed open the door and made a mad dash to the refrigerator. There it sat, brick solid in the wintry freezer. The wall clock warned that her mom would be home in half an hour. She dumped her stuff on the floor and grabbed hold of the meat. One vigorous tug and out shot the icy clump, propelling her into the wall. She tried drowning it in a sink of hot water to soften it up but the iceball core stubbornly resisted. If only they had a microwave. A short stay in the oven darkened the mound's surface but left a pink interior. Cameron decided that the only alternative was to hide the meat at the bottom of the trash can. She decided to be tired of chili.

She found the TV remote stuck between the lumpy cushions of the sofa. Typical afternoon fare flickered on the screen.

"Judge, believe me, I *swear* I paid her the back rent I owed. *She* the one who owe *me* money for them implants!"

Click.

"The lawyer's assailant remains at large and police are asking anyone with information to call the number at the bottom of the screen."

Click.

"Tammy, you're barely sixteen years old, you've already been arrested four times, you have two beautiful little kids . . . Look at your mother crying . . . Look at the studio audience . . . We all care, Tammy, but only *you* can—"

Click.

"Despite surging violence in the region, the President assured the nation in his news conference that an exit strategy . . ."

Click.

"I . . . I . . . I'm afraid, Chad, of being hurt again. But here you are standing before me in the flesh, that glorious flesh . . . Oh God, I don't care!"

Click.

There was nothing to watch. She might as well do homework.

"Hon, I'm here! Where are you? How was school? The chopped meat defrosted? *Caaa*meron!"

"In my room!" She shut her loose-leaf notebook and rolled onto her back. Reading assignments, writing projects, phone conversations, daydreaming, Cameron did it all sprawled on the linoleum floor. "Can we have pasta instead, Mom? I might be becoming a vegetarian!"

She found her mother counting out change. One look at her face and she knew the day's tips hadn't been good. Quarters, dimes, and nickels tumbled and rolled across the wobbly table. Customers were so stingy, she said, and they still had the nerve to be demanding. What a long, lousy friggin' day. She sent Cameron to the kitchen for something to prop up the table leg.

An empty Maypo box was in the trash. Cameron pulled it out, her brain buzzing. That table was forever going lopsided and whatever they put underneath the short leg eventually popped out. But it wasn't really surprising because all their furniture was bought used—already old, peeling, and cracked. The silverware drawer didn't close all the way, the sliding closet door was always derailing off the track, and that stained, gateleg table was the pits. Maybe she'd be a carpenter when she grew up and fix everything. But it had to pay well. If all you took home from a job was a handful of chump change and a grumpy mood, maybe you should look for another one. Once, she'd said exactly that to her mom. It was around Christmas, when, as usual, Patricia was working lots of extra hours so they could have a fancy tree, awesome presents, and special food. But it all got ruined by her mom's grouchy, tired mood. So Cameron made a suggestion—maybe she should find a better job, or a workaholic husband. How was she supposed to find a better job, her mom responded angrily, when she didn't even have a friggin' high school diploma? She ignored the husband part, on that she said nothing.

Cameron tore off the cereal box top and folded the cardboard strip into a small, thick square. After graduation from carpenter training school she'd join a union and pay their bills with her big paycheck and take them on awesome vacations to Atlantic City and Disney World and to see that leaning tower in Italy where her dad came from.

"What are you doing in there, hon, building a new table? My coins are sliding down a ski slope out here!"

Cameron reappeared, slipped the square under the leg, and got the table balanced.

"There ya go, ma'am, just like new. That'll be $24.99 for parts and labor for Cam's Carpentry, at your service."

Joking sometimes helped her mom's mood.

"Why thank you, Miss Carpenter." She placed a quarter on the steady table. "And here *you* go, paid in full." She slid a nickel across the table. "Plus tip."

Cameron felt good to see her mother laughing.

The dusky evening light tinted the kitchen a soft red. Patricia stood at the stove dangling a string of spaghetti into her mouth.

"Perfectly al dente. The sun-dried tomatoes and pesto ready?"

Cameron had cut the tomatoes into thin slices with a scissor and was stirring them into the warmed sauce.

"Yep."

"Table set?"

"Yep."

Patricia served the meal, turned on the evening news, and they sat down and ate to reports of smoke-filled subways, fatal carjackings, and miracle diets that really work.

"So what's this about you becoming vegetarian? I hope you're not getting mixed up in some kind of cult. You're not going anorexic, are you?"

"Right, Mom. Why do I have to be in a cult or anorexic? You're so dramatic, you and my living-arts teacher would get along great." She flashed guiltily on the meat in the trash can that she had ruined. "I said *might*. Anyway, I'm over it now."

"*That* fast?" asked Patricia. "It's only been a couple of hours. You're a real piece of work."

She drank some Hawaiian Punch from a bright lime plastic cup, the brilliant green accentuating her red nails. They dined as newscasters joked between grim stories, and commercials touted cars with personality, personal debt consolidation plans, and soothing remedies for acid reflux.

"Can I change channels?" asked Cameron, clicking the remote. "*The Shield*'s coming on. I *live* for that show."

"Mmm," grunted Patricia, her mouth full and her hand up as if to say "Stop."

"What?" Cameron clicked to the channel but got a blank blue screen. "What's going on?"

Her mother swallowed.

"No more cable, we can't afford it. I had to cancel it." She pursed her lips. "No big deal, there's plenty of regular channels."

"C'mon, Ma, you're kidding, right? How am I gonna watch *The Shield*? I *love* *The Shield* . . . "the road to justice is twisted" . . . I *need* *The Shield*. After high school I'm joining the Strike Team. Vic Mackey's totally *sick*."

"All the more reason for you not to be watching some sicko show."

"*Sick* meaning *awesome*. Come on, I'm begging!"

"It's called No, Cameron. We don't have the money. End of discussion."

Cameron slumped backward like a rag doll. *The Shield* was worlds cooler than everything else on TV. She liked how the cops were half-good and half-bad, not perfect but not evil either. Bummer! She was totally devastated forever. More moaning. There was nothing worth watching on other channels.

"Would ya stop that moaning, Cameron, for chrissakes, you sound like a wounded animal."

"*Maaa*, please, Ma." Cameron knew her mother never budged once her mind was made up, but she whined anyway.

"Cameron, *stop* it. Now, tell me about school. You get back on time? You had enough money for a tip? How was class?"

She grumpily recounted her afternoon. Mr. Robinson's stagy way of talking, Othello and Iago, the arguments about O. J. Simpson and Michael Jackson, the funny comments people yelled out in class, the discussion about dating. The tangle with the project girls in the mall was censored out since she was supposed to have gone directly home.

"So, Ma, would *you* ever go out with a black guy?"

Patricia began noisily collecting plates, knives, and forks.

"You're gonna wear me out with your million and one questions. Look at the time, you better go on to bed. You finish your homework?"

She gave her daughter a good-night kiss and went to the kitchen to clean up.

five

The fragrance of late springtime flowering trees and blossoming gardens held the promise of summer. Along the avenue old women, still in their winter coats, gathered at outdoor stands, tapping and sniffing fruits and vegetables. High schoolers crowded bagel stores and pizza shops, shouting orders and jostling one another.

The Storms kept to their routine of rushed mornings, busy days, and drowsy evenings. Most days, Cameron managed to arrive at school on time, unless she lost herself in the riffs and wails of an Evanescence song. Amy Lee had replaced Avril Lavigne in Cameron's sacred firmament of music stars, the thickly eyelined goth singer being worlds cooler than the colicky Canadian. Miss Goldstone forbade her to sit next to Amanda during tests but couldn't stop their covert text-messaging of questions and answers. Caught with a beer in the girls' restroom, P was suspended from school for a week and grounded at home for two. And all three mercilessly teased Crystal about the diner incident, quipping "G'head, girlfriend, act black" and "Wassup, playa?" and "Yo, Crys*taaal*, what's the 411?"

One evening, Patricia came home from work at the usual time but barely made a sound. No calling Cameron's name. No rattle of pans or clink of dishes. No newscaster's drone from the TV. Cameron cupped her ear and listened. Car motors hummed, passersby chatted, a baby cried, but not a noise from the other side of the door.

"Ma?"

Cameron sat up.

"Ma, you out there?"

She went to the living room, where her mother was lying down, her face to the back of the sofa. Cameron knelt on the floor.

"What's wrong?" Her heart was drumming. She shook her mom's shoulder delicately, as if she feared it might break. "Is everything all right?" With each question her voice grew softer until in a whisper she asked, "You okay, Ma?"

Patricia rolled over, her face trickling tears and mascara. Cameron had never seen her mother cry. The terrible sight silenced her.

"Honey, Elga's closing the salon. Not enough clients, too many taxes, she had a million and one excuses. The witch waited until today, Friday, to tell us not to come back on

Monday. You don't *do* that to people. She drives a Mercedes, has a big house over in Manhattan Beach, *blinds* you with her friggin' gold crosses and fancy jewelry." She uncrumpled the tissue in her hand and blew her nose. "I tell you, it was like cry me a river in there with me, Irina, Valya, Anna all boo-hooing our eyes out. They don't even have their green cards. Where're they gonna find work?"

Cameron's head filled with terrifying thoughts. Where would they get food? Would they have to sell their belongings on the sidewalk like some of their evicted neighbors had done? What if Mom couldn't pay her bills, would she go to jail? And with no mother around, what would become of *her*? She wiped her eyes.

"Don't cry, honey, everything will turn out all right. Elga says she owns another place right here in Brooklyn that has an opening. The job's mine if I want it. The salary won't be the same, it'll be lower, but still, nails are all I know and at my age changing careers . . ."

That piece of news eased Cameron's anxiety. Her mom still had a job! So why was she crying?

"There's something else. We may have to"—she paused— "I'm not gonna be able to afford this rent."

"We have to *move*?" Cameron swallowed. She was born here. She'd finally gotten her room set up right. Amanda, P, Crystal . . . her closest friends lived a few streets over. She didn't want to go anywhere else. She couldn't. She *wouldn't*. She'd run away!

"I'm afraid so, Cameron. The rents in this area have shot way up since I first moved in here with you and— since I first moved in here. We'll have to see what's out there. Elga knows people in real estate."

"But . . . but . . . what about school? I don't want to go to a different one now. All my friends are at Herbert Hoover."

"We'll get through this. I have a few dollars saved that'll tide us over for a while."

Cameron rested her head on her mother's arm. There they stayed for a long while, listening to the familiar noises of the neighborhood they might have to leave. That night Cameron spent hours on the phone with Amanda, then P, then Crystal. She even left a message on Toby's cell phone saying they could get back together. She needed something, someone solid.

On normal Saturdays when the weather was good, Cameron and the girls strolled around the neighborhood, checking out the cute boys and dissing the uglies. But things were far from normal on this Saturday, and the collective gloomy mood of Amanda, P, and Crystal cast a shadow over the sunlit weekend. All they talked about was what P called "the mother of all bummers." Cameron and Mrs. Storm were family, they *couldn't* leave the neighborhood. Amanda promised to ask her doctor-father to find Mrs. Storm a job at his hospital. P said her house had room for them both since one or the other of her feuding parents was always packing up and splitting for long periods. Crystal said they should rob a bank like the four girls in *Set It Off*.

Amanda sneered. "That's choice, Crystal, *dahhh*. So we'll *all* have to move—to prison? Nothankyouverymuch."

Cameron said she might run away from home and go live in the Brazilian rain forest.

P made a face. "I thought you wanted to stay with us. Now you're running off to some faraway leafy little forest full of exotic natives? If you gotta move, you gotta move. Just suck it up and do it. As long as you guys don't move to Queens."

No way, said Cameron, not corny Queens. Brooklyn was the best borough.

"Yeah," piped up Crystal, "and don't move to, like, Staten Island, where you can only go by boat because it's an island."

The others cringed.

"What do you think Manhattan *Island* is, Crystal?" asked P. "And Long *Island*, which Brooklyn, by the way, is part of? Do you row, row, row your boat there?"

Amanda added, "And have you ever noticed the four-thousand-foot ribbon of steel called the Verrazano-Narrows Bridge that connects Staten Island to the rest of the world?"

Picking on Crystal rather than dealing with Cameron's possible departure from the neighborhood made everyone feel better. Except Crystal.

"You know, I don't think it's right to gang up on a person every time she says something that isn't, like, perfect. I have really sensitive feelings." Her chin quivered as she spoke.

So did Cameron's, but for other reasons. She was going to miss them, know-it-all Amanda, rebellious P, crazy Crystal.

"Don't worry about those two nerds, Crys," said Cameron, putting her arm around Crystal. "They're nerds. Me and you, we'll rob a bank and take a cruise boat to Brazil."

They tried to come up with other solutions to Cameron's horrible plight but in the end settled for solving a much easier dilemma—the cable TV problem. It was agreed that they'd meet every week to watch *The Shield*. Amanda said that was the least true friends could do. Unwilling to imagine Cameron somewhere else, they spent the rest of the afternoon searching the neighborhood for rental apartments.

That evening, Cameron lay on the floor of her room staring at the ceiling. Next to her, the cell began trembling and spinning. "Tobias Richland" popped up in the phone window. She regretted leaving him a message and considered not answering. A flashback to that gross time in the gym with him grunting and squeezing her breasts like they were Stress Balls made her grimace. What was she *thinking*, calling him?

"Cam, waddup, it's me, Toby."

"I know, the phone shows who's calling."

"I'm chillin' with my folks at our crib on the North Shore. So, like, I got your message and *bam!* know what I'm sayin'?"

She yawned. "Yeah, you said bam."

"I'm talkin' shock city. But who loves you, baby, me and that's *word*. So yeah, let's *do* this. I'ma be back in the hood tomorrow and we'll hook up, me and you on the remix tip. It's gon' be hella good. So school me, what made you go from me and you 'fornever' to all of a sudden feelin' me?"

"Nothing. Bye."

Patricia was home all the time and she seemed really different, in a bummer kind of way. She stopped rushing Cameron to school in the mornings, which she spent in bed. And she wore these crazy clown outfits Cameron called "housefits"—plaid pajamas and striped housecoats—that she slept in and wore again the next day. If Cameron didn't run to the phone, it wasn't answered. Her mother stopped opening the mail. She no longer asked a string of questions when Cameron walked in the door. Rarely did she ask any at all. Once in a while Cameron would ask about the other job possibility and get no answer. Nothing made her mom feel better, not cracking jokes, not playing Evanescence real low, not even keeping her hair brushed down. But Cameron kept trying. She knew the days had all begun to look alike from the sofa, where her mom spent them, because she was always asking Cameron what day of the week it was. And any mention of the salon brought her to tears.

six

Alone in her salon, Elga Oblomovna packed wooden crates and taped cardboard boxes, tunelessly singing along with a recording of the St. Petersburg Russian Folk Orchestra. The place looked like a tornado had swirled through, toppling chairs, flipping tables, and trailing trash. Patricia pushed open the salon door, the breeze rolling clumps of dust across the floor. An odor of pungent perfume smacked her in the nostrils. Thoughts of Cameron gave her the resolve to face the wench.

"There she is, my dear Trisha! I was starting to wonder if maybe you didn't want your money. All the others came already for pay. Come, hold down this flap for me, please."

Elga Oblomovna was the kind of person who would inquire as to someone's well-being, then immediately begin talking about herself.

"How are you and little Cameroon?" she asked breezily.

"It's been hard but—"

"Oh, this moving is so much a nightmare for me, you cannot imagine, Trisha. My girls, Anna . . . Valya . . . Irina . . . that old Ludmila . . . oh, the vipers, the insects. I curse the graves of their ancestors. Not one has come to help, just Ukrainians wanting only money, money, money . . . no helping the other, no solidarity. Ah, my dear Trisha, if only you know how my heart breaks for the old ways when—"

"My check?" said Patricia drily.

"Of course, of course."

Patricia looked daggers at her back as Elga Oblomovna sauntered to her office, massive rolling hips under a cassock that looked like something from Tents 'R' Us. She returned and handed Patricia an envelope.

"I add little bonus for you. You're a good worker. The others"—she twisted her face into a frown—"lazy. Ukrainian."

Patricia was not interested in phony praise or two-faced put-downs.

"The job you mentioned, I'll take it if it's still available."

"Excellent, excellent! I held it for you only."

Lies poured from the woman like sewage from a burst levee. Patricia knew from Irina that each of them had been offered—and turned down—the low-paid position. Valya and Irina, pretty, bleached twenty-somethings, had immediately found work as hostesses in a local cabaret club. Anna was being kept by the young husband of a wealthy old client. Thanks to a well-connected associate of her late gunned-down husband, Ludmila was granted an "Empowering Women" government loan to open a Ukrainian Brides agency. She was also collecting unemployment, welfare, disability, and food stamps. Patricia was the only one who hadn't landed on her feet.

"Come to my office, Trisha, I give you all the information. A good opportunity, you will see."

Patricia's cell phone vibrated.

"Hi, Ma, it's me. How's it going?" Cameron was worried how her mom would react to being back at the salon.

"You're a love to call, hon. *I'm* the mother and you're checking on me. Your mom is A-OK, don't you worry. Now focus on whatever class you're in and I'll see you later."

"Cool. I can't wait to hear about the new job you might get. Call me when you leave, okay?"

The job Cameron wanted to hear about was at Elga Oblo-movna's other salon, Easy E's Nubian Nails. It was in a black neighborhood on the other side of Brooklyn, close to a public housing project. Elga Oblomovna rarely set foot in the area and ran the salon from what she considered a safe distance. The business was in the name of its manager, Ashaka John-son, which qualified it for low-interest loans and tax breaks reserved for minority-owned businesses. They'd met in a

Brooklyn police precinct, where Elga was being questioned on suspicion of money laundering and Ashaka was being booked for loitering.

The clients were mostly young and of color and the prices they paid significantly higher than at Madame Elga's. The employees were exclusively young and of color and the wages they received significantly lower than at Madame Elga's. It wasn't always the most serene place to work—the rap star Foxee Black had been arrested there for assaulting two salon workers over her bill.

Much of the above was left out of Elga Oblomovna's description to Patricia. She portrayed a lively workplace full of music and young energy in a neighborhood that had lots of nice fast-food restaurants. It was too bad about the salary, said Elga, but her money pressures were many. As for the neighborhood, well it *would* be a big, big change, but there was no need for Trisha to fear the blacks.

"I'm the last person who'd be afraid of black people," snapped Patricia, "so speak for yourself, Elga."

"No reason for a temper, my dear Trisha. I talk from my heart for you. Anyway, another very good thing for you is the work, much easier. Stick on nail tips, apply quick coat, and—bingo!—all finished. These people, they're different from Russians"—here she frowned again—"not so demanding. And they give you nice tip."

Patricia got the salon's address, price list, and the names of her new boss and co-workers. But what about the promised housing? If she couldn't find an affordable rent she was screwed, with or without a job.

"I need a cheaper place to live. You said you know people?" It galled her to ask that old Russian witch for help, but she had no choice.

"Ah, yes . . . You know, Trisha, Brooklyn used to be so cheap, now more expensive than Manhattan." She raised her eyes to the ceiling. "Look at me, how I struggle so hard to pay off my little shack. Rent, buy, no difference these days, everything cost too much." She lowered her voice. "But I know a man, Ukrainian but *good*, a *good* man. Is head of public housing for mayor's office. I already call him for you. So you give a little something to show appreciation, maybe a hundred, not more than a hundred fifty, and this man will put your name at very top of the long, long waiting list for projects not so far from salon."

The reaction was seismic. "Projects? Are you friggin' out of your Russian mind? I have a *child*, remember? A *teenaged girl*, for chrissakes! I sure as hell can't take her from our quiet neighborhood to some godforsaken housing project way out in *oombatzland*, full of God knows *what* kind of people. And I'm supposed to *pay* for the honor too? It's called thanks, but no thanks. You can't do us any better than *that*?"

A tone of impatience flashed in Elga's voice. "Sure, I do better. You got a thousand or sixteen hundred a month for rent?"

Patricia's angry pride stanched her tears. She marched out of the salon, slamming the tattered pink door.

"You're *welcome*, my dear Trisha!"

Patricia couldn't bring herself to call Cameron.

Over dinner, Patricia brought up the painful subject. They might—*might*—she said, have to think about public housing. Cameron lost it in a wail of tearful refusal. Projects?! She remembered the scary girls in the diner. No way. Patricia tried to console her and swore she'd do everything in her power to find them something else. Cameron was inconsolable.

Every morning with great determination Patricia pored over the rental ads in newspapers and checked listings on the Internet. She had friends watching out for an available place. She posted tear-off "1BR Apartment Sought" notices in laundromats, candy stores, shops, and restaurants. She even got down on her agnostic knees and prayed. It was one thing, she fumed to whatever deity was listening, to take a pay cut for the same work, but the Storms were not going to any housing project. There was still enough money for the next few months' rent, but soon there'd be none if she didn't start working right away.

It seemed like every morning Cameron came to breakfast with swollen eyelids. And Patricia always had dark bags under her eyes. But on this day, Patricia had smeared makeup on the bags. Slumping at the table, Cameron dragged her spoon back and forth in her cereal.

"Try to eat something. If you don't eat, you won't be able to pay attention in school."

"Not hungry."

Patricia tried to sound upbeat. "Today's the day your mother gets back in the working-woman saddle. Wish me luck!"

Cameron pushed away her bowl and stood. "Good luck," she said in a flat voice.

"Want me to call you on my lunch break and give you the scoop?"

"Sure, whatever."

Cameron left for school and Patricia called the salon for directions.

"Huh? I can't hardly hear you!" Ashaka clamped her hand over the receiver. "Would y'all turn down that monotonous ass 50 Cent! I can't hear a damn thing!" She pressed the phone to her ear. "Now what was you saying, miss? Directions?"

An hour and fifteen minutes later of subway riding, a bus transfer, and a four-block walk, Patricia arrived at Nubian Nails. Full of dread, she took a deep breath and rang the bell on the metal door.

"Name?" hollered a woman over the scratchy intercom.

"Patricia . . . Patricia Storm!"

"Patricia who? You not on the list! Did you make an appointment?"

"I'm the new technician from Madame Elga's! Is Ashaka Johnson in?"

"Yeah, she in, that's who you talking to!"

A buzz, a click, and Patricia stepped into her new place of work. Blasting rap music rang in her ears. The salon was mobbed with young people, some waiting in chairs along the walls, others sitting at about a dozen polish tables. She couldn't tell the clients from the employees, as no one wore the white smocks she was used to. What they *did* wear were elaborate hairdos, flashy jewelry, cleavage tops, and jeans that looked either too loose or too tight. A shapely young woman flaunting a diamond stud in her navel met Patricia at the door.

"It's about time, girl. Elga said a *while* ago that you was coming. You *see* we bustin' out in here with all these clients. But now ain't the time for chitchattin'." She called to an employee. "Asia, this is Pat! She new! Hook her up at a table!" And then to a client. "Hey, Boot-Boot, get your tail up, you next!"

Patricia took a seat while Asia prepared her workspace. She overheard snippets of conversation.

"So he gon' be like, 'What I did?' I was like, 'What you mean what you did? You damn well *know* what you did. Ask *her* what you did.' Then I just like, bounced."

This was going to be one hell of an experience. Her first client was already waiting. Boot-Boot was decked out in a glittery red midriff top, finely stitched designer jeans, and large square gold earrings. Her hair was a swirl of black and red braids. She sat down and Patricia took her hand.

"Hi, I'm Patricia . . . Pat. And you're . . . Boot . . . Boot? That's cute. It's a nickname?" She held the girl's slim hand in hers, inspecting the old, shoddily applied overlays.

"Uh-huh. It short for Bootaysha."

"Ohhh . . . Bootaysha . . . hmmm."

"You new, right? You got experience, I hope, 'cause, no offense, but I can't have no beginner messing up my nails."

"No need to worry about that, I've probably been doing nails longer than you've been alive."

"Nah, I don't *think* so . . . you how old?"

"Now, Boot-Boot, you know you shouldn't ask an old lady her age! We're sensitive."

"Come on, I'll tell you mine. I'ma be eighteen next Saturday. That's why I'm getting my nails done. For my party."

"All right. I'm thirty-eight but shhh . . ."

"No you ain't! You sure don't look it." She caught the eye of her friend seated against the wall. "Shaqualla! Over here, naphead! You owe me cash money! I *told* you she wasn't no forty years old! I wins! *Holla!*"

"How old she is?" shouted Shaqualla.

Everyone within earshot looked over to see who they were talking about. Patricia blushed from ear to ear.

"She thirty-eight but she keepin' it on the d-low!"

"Boot-Boot!" exclaimed Patricia. "For chrissakes."

"Girl, get out my face," said Shaqualla. "Ain't no difference between thirty-eight and forty! You ain't won nothin'!"

Boot-Boot turned in her chair to look her friend dead in

her face. "Shaqualla, don't *mess* with me. You *payin'* me my five dollars or you getting *served.*"

"Right. Serve *this.*" She held up three fingers. "Read between the lines."

The gesture made Patricia laugh, then she scolded the girl for announcing her age to the entire world.

It was nonstop laughter from that point on, and soon Boot-Boot was calling Patricia her "main girl" and telling lurid stories about her many "mens." When the work was done, she absolutely loved her peppermint-striped nails and pranced around with her hands stuck out, touting Patricia's "off tha hook skills."

At lunchtime most of them ate fast food at their tables, gossiping loudly, singing along with the music, sometimes jumping up to dance. Patricia took it all in, delighted and overwhelmed as she and Ashaka headed out for lunch at a Chinese take-out. The manager explained how things operated at the salon and complimented the quality of Patricia's work, which she said was better than any she'd seen. After lunch and before starting on a new client, Patricia called Cameron.

"Hi, Mom." Cameron sounded just as depressed as she had that morning.

Patricia tried to perk her up with descriptions of the crazy energy at work, the girls' personalities, the wild clients, the music. It was demanding but she had the feeling she was going to like it. Cameron said absently that she was glad to hear it, then said bye, class was starting.

The afternoon zipped by in a flurry of fingernail designs—leopards, flowers, butterflies. There seemed to be no limit to the clients' imaginations. One girl wanted a design showing her and her boyfriend "gettin' busy," which was where Patricia drew the line. The atmosphere in her new place of work was as refreshing as it was foreign. The salon crackled with energy and a kind of camaraderie that was new to her. The music would probably end up driving her out of her friggin' mind, but for the time being she was still sane and happy to have a job. Elga was right—these young, buoyant clients tipped better than Madame Elga's tightwads. By the time she arrived home, all she could do was flop on the couch and have Cameron bring her food.

seven

"SUP? WAN2TLK?" asked P.

Cameron sneaked a glance at her phone. Yes, she *did* want to talk, she messaged from her lap, keeping a wary eye on the teacher. It felt like someone had hijacked her life and tossed it upside down. Nothing was right anymore, nothing was sure. The home she'd grown up in, the school she assumed she'd graduate from, the friends who were supposed to always be there . . . everything was changing, and for the worse. Her mom no longer flip-flopped from mood to mood. Since starting the new job she stayed in *one* mood all the time—wiped. Which meant Cameron had to fix dinner. They ate lots of tuna melts, BLTs, and hamburgers. She most definitely wanted to talk.

"T+," said P.

Thinking positive was easy to say, but she'd try.

"SLAP," Cameron wrote back. *Sounds like a plan.*

Amanda kicked her foot and whispered, "Gallstone alert."

Ruth Goldstone was their strictest teacher and she hated inattention more than anything. At five feet tall, she was also the shortest. The big joke was for a tall kid to find a pretext to walk next to her, asking some bogus indentured servitude question about the Middle Ages, to accentuate her Lilliputian stature. But what she lacked in height, she made up for in attitude. Students watched their behavior in her class because they knew that in a second she'd lower a grade, phone a parent, or order them to guidance. Stealthily, she had made her way to Cameron's seat while the class was copying down the assignment.

"And just *what* are you fiddling with, Cameron Storm, or dare I ask?"

Cries of "nasty" and "perv" mixed in with a chorus of hoots.

"Uh . . . nothing," blurted Cameron, quickly tucking her phone away.

"Really? So what was that *nothing* you jammed in your pocket? As you well know, Herbert Hoover High has a rule against cell phone use in class."

"Nothing," said Cameron, resigned to being sent to guidance.

Miss Goldstone brought her mouth so close that Cameron felt the woman's moist breath on her cheek.

"Do you care so very little about the French Revolution, one of the most pivotal moments in European history, that you'd rather"—she raised her voice—"twiddle-twaddle around in your lap"—the students roared—"than learn about an important ally?"

Cameron jumped to her feet.

"I don't give a rat's ass about the floofie French or their stupid revolution! Screw them, screw you, and totally screw Herbert Hoover!"

In the startled moment that followed, Miss Goldstone's face turned ashen. The only sound heard was that of a truck rattling down the street. Cameron ran from the room, whoops and applause rising at her back. Livid, Miss Goldstone whipped out her own cell phone and called Mr. Siciliano on the spot.

P stepped from the girl's restroom as Cameron was coming down the corridor.

"Cam! Sweets!" she called excitedly, waving.

Cameron did a U-turn. Her cheeks were flushed and wet.

"What the hell happened, Cam?"

By way of answer, Cameron just shook her head.

"Come on," said P, pulling her into the restroom.

P sat on the sink and Cameron slid down the wall onto the floor.

"Here," offered P, "you look like you could use a sip."

Cameron pushed away the silver flask. "You're gonna end up in AA."

"I'm not worried, my folks are drinkers. It's in the family. Anyway, look at the French, they drink all day."

"Screw the French. Buncha winos."

"More like whin*ers*," sniped P. "The wimps didn't even support us in the war even though we saved them from the Nazis in World War II. It was on the History Channel."

"I hate them because Gallstones worships them." Cameron was shredding a roll of toilet paper she'd picked up.

P popped a toy-truck-red jellied thing in her mouth.

"Ewww, what's that?"

"Chuckles," said P, chewing. "Want one?"

"Gross. They are like *so* fattening."

P ate another of the sugarcoated candies, this one synthetic yellow.

"No, they're not. Whatever you eat with love turns to protein in your body. And I *love* Chuckles."

"Right."

"Whatever. I wanna know about *you*, what's going on?"

Cameron told her.

P blamed herself for sending the text message. She wanted to go to Gallstone's class right then and pound that midget into the floor. "Not for nothing, but you know how when a boy likes you, he'll scribble insults on your locker, dis your outfit, punch you in the shoulder?"

"Yeah. And?"

"Well, Miss Gallbladder probably has a secret crush on you. I mean, who's not married at *her* age? That's why she's so on your case."

"Jeez, ewww. You should smell her breath!"

Cameron stood, stretched, and hopped up on the sink

next to P. Screw Gallstones. What was really bothering her was the move.

"I don't know what I'm gonna do if we have to move way out to oombatzland. I'll *die* in the projects. Me, a *white* girl. I'll die."

"No, you won't. You'll suck it up and deal. It's not like we won't be friends anymore. Me, you, Amanda, Crystal—we're sisters for life." She struck a pose, arms folded across her chest, head cocked to one side. "Word is bond, know what I'm sayin', sistagirl? You bein' up in da hood ain't changin' a *damn* thing." She dropped the pose. "Now *do* it and *like* it."

As they explored the pros and cons, Cameron began to feel better. P could make her feel able to face anything, no matter how trippy. P was awesome that way.

A hall monitor stepped into the bathroom.

"*What* are you girls doing in here?" The woman scrutinized them over the top of her glasses.

"Peeing," answered P with a straight face.

"In the sink?" She sniffed the air like a bloodhound.

"No, ma'am, we needed a bidet. Like the French."

Cameron burst into uncontrollable laughter.

The woman gestured toward the door. "Get outta here and go to class before I write you both up."

The next morning, Mr. Siciliano summoned Cameron straight out of homeroom. The office door was open when she got there.

"Have a seat."

His tone was serious. Cameron felt her stomach cringe.

"You'll probably not be surprised to know that your behavior yesterday seriously upset your teacher, and disrupted the class."

"Oh, right. She's the one who started it by making fun of me."

"Miss Goldstone said you were messaging on your cell phone during class and when she reminded you of the school's telephone policy, you used profanity and left class without permission. These are serious infractions, Miss Storm."

"I *so* did not use profanity, Mr. Siciliano! Screw's not a curse."

"You also referred to the ass of a rat. 'Ass' is a profanity."

"No, it's not, it's a donkey!"

He began filling out a form. "I'm going to have to suspend you for—"

"Mr. Siciliano . . . wait . . . This is totally so unfair! Miss Gall— Goldstone's always picking on me for no reason. You can't suspend me. Suspend *her*."

He continued writing.

"Why won't you listen to me?" Cameron's breath was coming in short gasps. She *couldn't* get suspended from school on top of everything else! It would *kill* her. And her mom!

The counselor slapped his desk.

"Why won't I listen to you? I *do* listen to you, Miss Storm, I listen to every ridiculous tale you bring in here! First it's a lunatic bus driver, now it's a hate-filled teacher—"

"But she *does* hate me! In front of the whole class she made it seem like . . . like . . . I was masturbating!"

Cameron burst into tears. Mr. Siciliano dropped his pen and snatched a tissue from a box on his desk.

"What?! Here, don't get yourself all worked up. Tell me truthfully, what, exactly, did she say?"

Sniffling and blowing her nose, Cameron went on. "She . . . she said I was . . . twi . . . twiddling or twaddling myself, something like that, and everybody was laughing." More tears flowed, rolling down her cheeks, under her chin and onto her Evanescence T-shirt. She couldn't stop.

"If Miss Goldstone made such an . . . inappropriate . . . comment, I'll certainly have a word with her. That's a promise. Now please . . . stop crying . . . Let me get you some water."

Mr. Siciliano filled a small paper cup. Cameron drank it straight down and wiped her mouth on the back of her shaky hand.

"I'm not suspending you, okay?"

She dabbed her eyes with a napkin.

"It doesn't matter," she sniffed. "I won't be here for long anyway."

"Don't *talk* like that, Cameron. You're fifteen years old, you have your whole life ahead of you. Suicide is not—"

"I don't mean *that*, jeez, I'm not *that* backward. I meant my mom can't afford our rent anymore and if we move, I'll have to go to a different school."

Hearing her own words made her cry some more.

"I'm sorry to hear that, really I am. You have your issues, but you're a good kid. It's a shame because your grades—and your punctuality—are showing some improvement. Where're you moving?"

She had another burst of tears.

"Come on, Cameron . . ." He patted her shoulder.

"To the *projects!*" she wailed, doubling over.

"Hey . . . hey . . ." The counselor raised her up by the shoulders. "Public housing isn't the end of the world. There are good people there just like anywhere else, and some bad, just like anywhere else. And even if you're outside the district, you might be able to finish up high school here at Hoover. We *do* take kids from elsewhere, you know. I can check that for you."

She bolted upright, her face bright with hope.

"Really? I don't care how long the bus ride is! If I can stay here with my friends, that would be so awesome!"

"Now let's not get ahead of ourselves, one step at a time. I'll check with the Board of Ed. In the meantime, I want you to feel that you can talk with me anytime, not just when you're sent here by a teacher."

They both got up.

"Thanks, Mr. Siciliano."

"You're very welcome, Miss Storm."

She shook his hand, picked up her knapsack, and turned to leave.

"By the way," he said at the door in an almost conspiratorial voice, "I'm from the projects myself . . . Hartford, Connecticut . . . Nelton Court in the house. You'll be okay."

The overdue rent forced Patricia to make a very hard decision. She agreed to pay the mayor's housing authority chief sixty-five dollars—and not a dime more—and he inserted their name at the top of the three-year waiting list for a two-bedroom in Marcus Garvey Gardens. Within weeks she'd received an acceptance letter. Instead of joy, the Storm home ran with tears, Cameron sprawled on her bedroom floor and Patricia fetal on the couch. Then began the ordeal of packing, discarding, donating, and cleaning.

Cameron packed dozens of CDs. She rolled her wall posters and eased them into cardboard tubes. She delicately untaped her precious pictures from the mirror. Jeans and sneakers, socks and underwear, baseball caps all dumped in one trunk; coats, jackets, and sweaters in another. Next came her tops. Evanescence's "Fallen" T-shirt, Avril Lavigne's "Don't Try to Tell Me What to Do," No Doubt's "Rock Steady," Nirvana's "Smiley," her "Enter at Your Own Risk"—all the T-shirts from her prized collection were folded carefully and placed in a special suitcase. Once the schoolbooks, stuffed animals, and CD player were boxed, she was done. Cross-legged in the middle of the floor, she surveyed what had been her refuge. The final tears shed, she got up and went to help her mother.

There, the packing effort had slowed to a standstill, but her mom wasn't standing. The bed was a jumbled heap of clothes, costume jewelry, nail technician training manuals, boxes of nail polish, high heels, toiletries, photo albums—and wedged in a narrow space lay Patricia, sound asleep. Cameron watched her mom's chest rise and fall like ocean waves. Her hair was a mess, her mouth slightly open, her arms awkwardly angled like those of a broken doll. Gently, Cameron draped her mother with a sheet, clicked open the suitcase on the floor, and began filling it with clothes.

eight

The new tenants stood close together in the lobby of Building A at Marcus Garvey Gardens, suitcases and boxes securely behind their legs. A ramp for the handicapped cut in half the little walking space there was, and a Tenant Patrol table, manned by a pair of spunky septuagenarians, blocked half the rest. Children chased each other round and round the hallway. Bowed women, stout with age and mettle, pulled squeaky-wheeled shopping carts of groceries. Babies in tiny warm-up suits and Nikes snuggled in the arms of their teenage mothers. Boys in baggy clothes and do-rags swaggered, sometimes cutting a loaded look Cameron's way.

"I'm going gray waiting for this friggin' elevator," mumbled Patricia, wiping her sweaty forehead, "and it's hot as hell in here. Don't you want to put that down?"

"Nope," said Cameron, gripping the handle of her special

suitcase. If anything got stolen, it was most definitely *not* going to be her T-shirts.

A woman with smooth, dark skin and a shock of white hair was waiting a few feet away. Cameron read with amusement her white T-shirt: "Black Don't Crack."

"Take a look at *my* hair. That's from waiting for this slow-as-molasses elevator for fifty-five years. You the people moving into 12-G, right?" This she said more like a statement of fact than a question.

"That's us, and you have a beautiful head of hair," responded Patricia, glad that the neighbors were friendly.

"What a right nice thing to say, Miss . . ."

"Storm, Patricia Storm. And this is my daughter, Cameron."

"Well, welcome to the Gardens, not that there's a single flower or speck of green for miles. That Housing Authority do absolutely nothin' for us. Now, don't be frettin' about being white, everybody get along just fine for the most part, seeing that we *all* poor. I'm Elvira B. Hutton but they call me Miss Vi."

A screech and a bump announced the elevator's arrival. The number of people piling out implied that the space inside was large, but once aboard with their belongings the Storms exchanged uneasy looks.

"Sugar," said Elvira, addressing Cameron, "press 8 for me, would you? Pretty as a little princess, ain't you?" She paused, contemplating the girl through thick glasses. "Put me in mind of my grandchild."

Not sure how to respond, Cameron said thanks. Then, "Your shirt's really cool. What does it mean?"

Elvira threw her hand over her mouth. "Child, you near made my teef pop out!" She was giggling like a kid. "How old you think I am, honey? How 'bout you, Patricia, you give me how old?"

Cameron figured the woman was probably really old, like around fifty, so she opted for the polite lie.

"I can't tell."

Patricia took in the woman from head to toe. Mid- to late sixties, she figured, but to be nice, said, "I'd say not a day over sixty."

Bing! chimed the elevator. They were at 8. Elvira shuffled toward the open door, a proud grin on her face.

"I'ma be seventy-six years young my next birthday! But it don't show 'cause black don't crack." She pinched Cameron's cheek. "That's what it mean, sugar. Now you have a nice day, you hear. And don't be no strangers. I'm in 8-A and I loves company."

When the elevator creaked to a stop at 12, Patricia was still marveling over how young Miss Vi looked and Cameron was imagining cute sayings for a shirt, maybe something like "White Stays Light" or "White Feels Right."

The graffitied door slid open and a monstrously brawny

pitbull lunged forward. A prong collar and a muscular arm were all that prevented the dog from mauling them.

"Down, blue bastard!" shouted the boy, whipping the animal's broad head with the end of the leash.

Shielding themselves behind suitcases as they quickly unloaded their stuff, Patricia and Cameron made it through the hall to the G apartment. Safe inside, they didn't smell the fresh paint or see the stunning Manhattan skyline in the distance because both were in tears.

"Ma," cried Cameron, "I can't do this!"

"*Yes*, we can," wept Patricia, "and we will."

During the succeeding days, furniture was delivered and bus and subway routes learned. They ventured into local stores. They were assured by a neighbor that the vicious blue pitbull and its brutal owner were rare visitors to their floor. Elvira visited often, leaving with pretty flowers on freshly polished fingernails.

Cameron's bedroom, larger than the one at their house, was arranged to her liking. Posters and pictures were up, the CDs organized alphabetically, and her T-shirts neatly hung in the roomy closet. Still, she struggled to adapt to the world outside her room. Mr. Siciliano had kept her enrolled at Herbert Hoover and she remained close to her old friends. But she hadn't made any new ones. Maybe she *should've* switched to the neighborhood school. She saw kids noticing her going in and out of the building, but few people spoke other than the occasional person who mistook her for a Latina and addressed her in Spanish. Amanda and P kept promising to do a sleepover one weekend but they hadn't showed up yet. Crystal was scared to visit but would, she said, if they all went together. Living in a black neighborhood made Cameron feel like an extraterrestrial. She wasn't used to the kind of music that thumped constantly through the walls, the way kids dressed, how they talked—it was like being on another planet. Her grades were sliding back down, but at least Miss Gallstones had stopped bothering her and no longer even looked in her direction.

"Here it is," said Patricia, knocking at a door adorned with a pair of fluorescent hands clasped in prayer. Miss Vi welcomed her dinner guests, a soulful croon floating out of the apartment.

"Hello! The food was getting lonely waiting on you two."

Patricia led the way, followed by Cameron, who'd tried every excuse to get out of dinner at Miss Vi's. The only other time she'd gone, she felt totally bored. Plus, the apartment was suffocating because the old woman was always chilly and kept the windows closed. They were standing just inside. The place was more overheated than usual from the morning's cooking, and Cameron wiped sweat from her eyebrows.

"What a gorgeous voice," said Patricia, hearing the music. "Who is it?"

"You don't know Sam Cooke, sugar? The man sings like a warm Southern breeze."

More like a scorching wind, thought Cameron, dabbing her moist forehead with her sleeve.

Worn linoleum covered the floor, curling uncooperatively in corners. They weaved past see-through plastic storage boxes, stacks of old *Ebony* magazines, hanging organizers crammed with heavy-soled shoes, and an overloaded laundry basket spilling shabby DD-cup bras. Cameron slid onto a wooden chair. She wanted to be a good neighbor and every-thing, but all she could think about was being upstairs in her room listening to her own music. Patricia plumped down on a green vinyl chair, its seat held together with heavy-duty wrapping tape. A bouquet of dusty plastic flowers decorated the round dining table Elvira had laid with three dishes of steaming food.

"Smells good, Miss Vi. For the life of me, I still can't get my catfish as crisp as yours. And look at that macaroni and cheese! I'll never be able to eat it from the box again. Please, sign me up at your cooking school. I'm the Overcooked Pasta Champion of Brooklyn."

Cameron agreed with a laugh. "Mom tries, but she never gets it right."

Elvira forked collards onto her own plate.

"You ladies sure enough gonna starve to death if you waiting for me to dish you up. Go on and help yourself, my days of serving white people ended a *looong* time ago."

They ate, drank, and chatted about goings-on in the Gardens. Cameron just sat, not taking part in the conversation. Her mind wandered. She imagined her girls on the other side of Brooklyn, sipping ice-cream sodas in an air-conditioned diner. Elvira treated them to the refined, subdued sound of Roberta Martin, the sanctified trilling of Rosetta Tharpe, and the pure power and vibrancy of Mahalia Jackson. The music stopped.

"Would you be so kind . . . ?"

"Of course, no problem." Patricia stepped carefully through the living room, a jumble of knickknacks that included a black lawn jockey. She stopped dead in her tracks.

"Miss Vi!"

"Don't tell me them roaches back again! That exterminator was in here not even a week ago."

Cameron nearly gagged on her food.

But there was nothing crawling. What had astonished Patricia was what was sitting on the step stool.

"A record player with a vinyl record album? Holy canoli, I didn't think there were any left. Cam, come look!"

"Wow, they still make those?" asked Cameron. "The CDs are so huge."

Patricia lifted the arm and gingerly placed the needle on *Sam Cooke's Greatest Hits.*

Elvira sang words she knew by heart. " 'Shake it like a bowl of soup / And make your body loop de loop . . . !' Now that's a tune to take you way back," she reminisced.

It was time for dessert. Elvira's homemade chocolate cake looked good, but Cameron felt like a water balloon. Looking at her mother, she said, "It's . . . uh . . . too hot for dessert."

Elvira shook her head. "Well, that's a new one on me! Too hot for dessert and summer's not even here yet."

The woman slipped back into her memories. "Me and my late husband, Odell, burning up that old Lafayette Ballroom dance floor down in Tuscaloosa . . . He was a handsome devil, my Odell, a real ladies' man too, that is till I straightened him out." Her milky eyes were full of the past.

Patricia watched her. "I can just see you dancing like a house on fire. If you don't mind my asking, how did your husband . . ."

"He had sugar. Lost one leg, the other, then his whole life to that wretched diabetes. People tried to fix me up with every Tom, Dick, and Harry they could find, but I never re-married, why would I? I had me the best man there was. Left me a good widow's pension too, from the United States Postal Service." She wiped a paper napkin across her lips. "How 'bout you?"

Patricia glanced at Cameron. "*That*, Miss Vi, is a long story. Or I should say, a short one." She took a moment to wipe her mouth, then said to her daughter, "Hon, seems like you're done eating. Go on back upstairs, I'll be up soon."

Cameron rose, thanked Miss Vi, and was gone.

As she locked the door, Elvira resumed her conversation. "My Odell. Now *that* was a good man, a good, faithful man."

nine

Upstairs, Cameron was looking for something to do. With no cable there wasn't much to watch on TV, and she'd already done her homework. She noticed a couple of taped boxes in her mother's bedroom. Poor Mom. With those crazy hours at the salon, there wasn't time for much else, not even getting her room together. Finishing the unpacking would be a nice surprise.

The bigger box was jammed with terry cloth towels, gloves, packs of fake fingernails, bottles of polish, jars of oils, and packages of exfoliating crystals. Cameron dragged it to the cabinet where Patricia kept work supplies and neatly filled the shelves. Next, she opened the smaller box and lifted out a bunch of magazines and newspapers. Tucked under them was a small photo album. Her mother had a number of albums with pictures of relatives, friends, Cameron at different ages, but this one she'd never before seen.

The printed cover was decorated with rows of little yellow baby chicks. On the inside title page was handwritten "Pat and Dante + Baby." The book held only four pictures in its plastic sleeves. The first was a black-and-white photo booth strip of her mom kissing some bushy-haired guy. The next one is her mom and the same guy smiling in front of a tray of hot dogs, fries, and drinks at a Nathan's outdoor picnic table. She's wearing a white hairband, a Hawaiian print top, and light blue overalls. He looks black. The third photo shows her mom cradling a baby in a hospital bed and the black man leaning into the photo with a grin. Cameron's hands tremble. She *knows* in her gut what she's seeing, but the words haven't yet reached her brain. For a long time she stares at the very last photo in the album. In it, she's in a baby blanket cuddled in her father's lap, Patricia looking on with a big smile.

Cameron's face was a dark, fiery red as she slowly closed the book of photos. Then she opened it and studied them a second time. Then closed it. Then reopened it to the photo of her as a baby with her father . . . Dante. Dad. He wasn't Italian, he was black. Omigod! African-American. Oh . . . my . . . God. Were they married? Divorced? What happened to him, where was he, *who* was he? Why didn't Mom ever *say* anything?! She remembered how she had changed the subject when Cameron asked if she'd date a black guy, how she always dodged questions about a man in her life.

Cameron closed the album and buried it in the box beneath the magazines and newspapers. She went to her room and dropped backward onto the bed. Her head was hurting really bad. Thoughts bounced back and forth between two shocking truths. She had a father. That father was black. A black father. It was too much, too much to take in at once. Dazed, she approached the mirror and studied her reflection. Thick, unruly curls . . . like his. Blue eyes . . . like her mom's. She looked at the faces of her idols—Avril, Britney, Gwen, Hilary . . . Mariah. Mariah's entrancing gaze seemed to hold hers, enter her being. Mariah was black because her father was. So wouldn't that make *her* black too? Mariah was trying to convey something to her, what was it? Transfixed, she moved closer to the singer's picture, her eyes desperate. Phrases swirled in her head . . . *the noble Moor of Venice, thick-lips, sooty, an old black ram . . . Everybody wants to be black these days . . . She looks white as us and that's what it goes by . . . That's ridiculous, it goes by your parents . . . Y'all white girls dissin' us?* Cameron's eyes rolled and she fell to the floor.

Moments later, Patricia unlocked the door and stepped inside.

"Hon, I'm back!" No response. "Cameron!"

She pushed open the bedroom door and found her daughter lying on the floor.

"Cameron?"

Cameron didn't respond.

"Cameron!"

She scooped her up. Cameron's eyes opened.

"What happened? You scared the friggin' daylights outta me!" She kissed Cameron's forehead again and again. "You all right? Say something." Tenderly, she helped her onto the bed, cupping Cameron's hands in her own.

"How'd you fall, honey, was it the heat? It *is* hot in this room. You should've eaten more. You sick? You got a temperature?"

Cameron could barely contain the shock waves roiling inside of her.

"How could you hide him from me, Ma?" Her voice sounded shrill, like someone else's.

Patricia flinched as though socked in the stomach. "What"—she fought to keep calm—"in heaven's name are you talking about?" But she knew exactly what Cameron was talking about, and a wave of guilt washed through her.

"I *saw* them, the pictures of you, me, and my dad! 'Pat and Dante plus baby,' remember? Why didn't you tell me? My whole life I thought I didn't have a father, that he was dead or missing or just never was. I hated Father's Day, kids bragging about doing stuff with their dads, and me feeling sick. If anybody asked about *my* father, I said I was a test-tube baby."

Her mother held Cameron's hands tighter as though to keep her from flying away.

"Cam . . . hon . . . I am so sorry, I had no idea. You never said anything about—"

"To who? You? Miss We-don't-discuss-that! Just because

he wasn't good enough for you doesn't mean I wouldn't have liked him. And even if he wasn't great, a bad dad's better than *no* dad!"

Cameron fell backward on the bed, covering her face, sobbing. Her stunned mother searched for the words that would make a teenage girl understand a broken heart and a cheating man, an unexpected pregnancy and a vanishing act.

Haltingly, she spoke of a young guy in a club who charmed her with his quick wit and good looks. Dante Hickman. At the time, he was nineteen and in college, or so he claimed, and she was a twenty-three-year-old waitress. They started seeing each other. He claimed to be a student at Brooklyn College. It turned out he wasn't. He supposedly lived with his parents in Jersey City. He didn't. When she got pregnant, he promised to marry her and help raise their child. He lied. He showed up at the hospital after Cameron's birth, seemingly happy. They found a house and moved in together. And then one day he left supposedly for school and she never saw him again. Brooklyn College had no record of a Dante Hickman and there was no trace of the Hickman family in all of New Jersey. End of story, one too painful to remember. So she blocked him out of her mind and out of Cameron's life.

"*That's* why my hair's like this! *That's* why I tan darker than everybody else! *That's* why I'm always reminding black people of some family member! I'm supposed to be white but

I'm really black! Is that why you didn't say anything, because you were ashamed of him . . . of me?"

For the first time, Patricia began to doubt her decision, but she felt certain about her motives. It wasn't about hiding the *color*—in this day and age a mixed kid was no big deal. It was about erasing the *man*, all of him.

"Absolutely not! I loved your father and I love you. Honey, you're *Cameron*, my beautiful daughter. Your father's black, yes. I'm white, yes. That makes you not one or the other but both."

Cameron rolled over, her back to her mother, and lay still, holding her head. Patricia sat for a long time just looking at her.

Cameron couldn't make sense of her thoughts. Her own mother had lied to her for years. Maybe not outright but by keeping silent. Was a secret the same thing as a lie? She didn't know the answer, but she sure *felt* the same way she did when someone lied to her. She was angry. She wanted to scream and yell. Throw and break things. But before she could do anything like that, the anger would morph into a sadness worse than any she'd ever felt. She couldn't get over it. All this time, she'd had a father. One who maybe would've really liked her and taken her out on birthdays, carried her on his shoulders at parades, called her his "baby girl." But she was gypped, robbed of all that because her mother had *issues*. Maybe it was just greed. Her mother wanting her all to herself. But what about what *she* never even got a chance to want—her dad?

Cameron was crying when Patricia tapped on the door.

"Lemme alone!"

Night fell and Cameron lay in bed fidgeting. She typed out a message for Amanda on her cell, then erased it. She left one for P but didn't say what she really wanted to. She dialed Crystal's phone number then hung up before it rang. She wrestled with the need to redefine herself. Black? White? Biracial? She sank into a fitful sleep.

On the other side of the wall, Cameron's mother sat upright on a chair holding an old photo album of miserable memories. Did the pain of that failed fling drive her, perhaps wrongly, to deprive her daughter not only of a father but of a heritage? She looked at the photo of the three of them, a handsome mixed family. In appearance, at least. But Dante left *them*, disappearing after the birth of his own daughter. He was the one who sure as hell took *himself* out of Cameron's life. Slowly, she turned the page. The playful young couple in the camera booth photos certainly *looked* happy enough to last more than a few months. He liked to jokingly call himself Dante's Inferno. That joke, as it turned out, was on her.

What *should* she have done? Cameron looked white, or maybe off-white, and had blue eyes. At the time they lived in a working-class neighborhood that was mostly white,

Cameron's friends were white, her *mother* was white, the world saw her as white. What good would it have done to rock the race boat? She leaned back in the chair. There was the hair, exactly like Dante's, the smile, also like his, certain mannerisms. Perhaps she *should've* tried harder to track him down, if only so Cameron might know her black grandparents, aunts, uncles, cousins. Know the rest of who she was. But who could say if *they* would've wanted to know *Cameron*?

Patricia dozed off that night to an uneasy sleep.

Days blended into weeks. At home, Cameron sulked. She promised herself to never in a hundred years speak to her mother again. At dinnertime, she ate in her room, listening to music. Once or twice she thought she heard the sniffling sound of someone crying, but she'd just turn the music up. In school, her friends tried to find out why she was acting so weird, but she said nothing. Teachers noted the change in her behavior—more argumentative, less prepared for class—and one of them decided to find out what was wrong. Sage Brown, the multicultures teacher Cameron really liked, signaled to her.

"Cameron, got a minute?"

"Not really, Sage."

The young woman took her by the arm. "Oh, come on, you don't have one little minute to spare for your hardworking teacher?"

They sat, the teacher on her desk, the student at a desk chair.

"I just wanted to check in, take your temperature."

Cameron studied her palm.

"Right," continued Sage. "So, Cameron, what's bothering you? Judging from the clucking and hissing noises you've been making lately, everything anyone says in class, including me, pisses you off."

"I'm sorry, Sage, I don't mean to be—"

"Hold it, we're not here for that, no apologies please. You're entitled to your feelings, I just want to know where they come from. Man problems?"

She wished Sage could see into her thoughts and spare her having to voice them. "In a way."

"In *that* you're not alone, Cameron," she said, shaking her head. "So tell me about it . . . him."

Between a torrent of tears and coughs, Cameron sputtered out the story of her father's existence and her mother's betrayal. She didn't mention the other part of the story because she hadn't yet figured out what it meant about *her* to be a black man's daughter. Overnight, she'd become some Cameron other than the one she'd always been. Besides, Sage was black. How would she react to some white girl saying she was suddenly black?

Cameron was surprised by how long she talked. A minute became a few, then several. The school bell rang and still she went on, recounting the questions gone unanswered by her mother, a little girl's Father's Day tears, the man on the beach with his daughter. And Sage listened, nodding occasionally. A half hour later, Cameron let out a "whew!," exhaled, and was done. She felt relieved, and her teacher hadn't said a word. When she did, Cameron became the one nodding in agreement.

"I understand completely how you feel, and it makes sense to me now why you've been so . . . ornery. What a double whammy! Finding a father and losing trust in a mother. You know, though, sometimes in trying to protect us, our parents do the opposite of what we'd want and what they should do. But don't be too hard on your mother. I have no doubt that she acted from a loving place. No more silent treatment, okay? You both have to work through this together—I'm sure she feels just as bad as you, if not worse—and that means talking. Okay?"

"Okay."

"And know that I'm here, okay?"

"Okay." Something made her go in a direction she hadn't planned to. "There's another thing I want to tell you . . . He's black . . . My dad's a black guy."

Sage slid down from the desk and took the seat next to Cameron.

"Wow. That's deep. Very deep. This is so much more than simply discovering a parent who's been hidden from you.

This flips, flops, and scatters to the wind your whole identity. You might need some help with this . . . What about Kennia Twist?"

Cameron had seen the school psychologist—once. It was first year, her grades had nosedived, and she felt like a mutant. But Miss Twist's nosy questions about periods and sex had completely grossed her out and she'd left in the middle of the session.

"Twisted Tran-sister? No way."

Sage found the nickname comical.

"You kids are so inventive, I love it. But seriously, I won't pretend to know what you're feeling. That's one complication I haven't had to deal with in my life. But I *do* have black friends with one white parent and they've been all over the emotional map. How're *your* friends reacting?"

"They're not. They don't know. Yet."

For a while they talked friendship and loyalty, difference and individuality, and then Sage had to get going. Cameron gave her a big hug and went home. She hoped her mom would try to strike up a conversation when she got in from work. She missed their talks.

ten.

Cameron was waiting at the dinner table when her mother got home. With as much nonchalance as she could muster, she greeted her with a warm "Hi, Mom, hungry? I made pasta."

Patricia had been giving her daughter as much breathing room as possible. She didn't argue when Cameron chose to eat behind closed doors, she didn't complain when Cameron didn't want conversation. She had decided to stay out of the way until Cameron was ready. She was.

"Mom, I know I've been kinda hardcore . . . I'm sorry."

"Honey, you have nothing to be sorry about, not a thing. If you only knew how sorry I am."

Eating together at the table for the first time in a while felt good to them both. Cameron continued the conversation she had begun with Sage. She was ready not only to talk to her mother but to face the most confusing question in her head.

"So like, am I black now?"

Patricia thought a while before answering. She wanted to do—and say—the right things this time.

"Well, the way I understand it, at least according to what your father told me, is that it used to be that a drop of so-called black blood meant you were black. They called it the one-drop rule. But I don't think people go by that anymore. Look at Tiger Woods."

"He's black."

"That's not what *he* says. He invented his own race, what was it? . . . Cablinasian. Caucasian, black, Indian, and Asian. With you, it's a lot simpler. Other people might call you biracial. I call you my baby girl."

"So what do I tell my friends? Amanda, P, Crystal, they think I'm white like them."

"You *are* white like them. In part."

"But I'm black too."

Patricia squeezed Cameron's hand. "That's exactly it. You're black *too*, not black *period*."

Cameron devoured computer Web sites dedicated to bi-, tri-, and multiracial people. Some claimed both their mom's and their dad's race, some went with one or the other, others insisted on their individuality. One night, she was almost bouncing on the couch, breathlessly reciting names and origins. There was Slash, the guitarist from the original Guns N' Roses—his mother was black, his father, white. And the newscaster Suzanne Malveaux, Yankees baseball star Derek Jeter, and basketball star Jason Kidd—black fathers, white mothers. And a singer named Shirley Bassey—half English, half Nigerian. And a famous concert pianist, André Watts—black and Hungarian. And the actor Vin Diesel, black, Italian, German. And The Rock and Sade and Senator Barack Obama and Sean Paul, all mixed. Even the totally blond TV star Heather Locklear was part black! Cameron felt the bud of a new self emerging, one that was richer, rounded, colorful.

"All right, *all right*, hon, I gotcha! There's a million and one mixed people in this world and you're in good company."

"Some of them look black and some totally white. When I first found out about Dad I felt so scared, like I wasn't Cameron anymore but someone from an alien nation. But now I'm really excited. I'm me and *more*. I only wish he'd stayed around, so I could've seen, I don't know, what a dad, *my* dad, was like. And the other part of my family too, his part. That would've been awesome."

"I know," said Patricia in a subdued voice. "I wish he'd stayed around too. But you know what, your mother did."

Cameron fell silent. Yes, her mom *had* stayed around. And was still there. She thought about how sad it must've been to be ditched and left with a little baby—her—to raise alone. But her mom had brought her home, found a job, supported them. That was pretty awesome too.

"I love you, Mom."

"I love you too."

"I know."

The atmosphere in the Storm household lightened up. Cameron felt like she was getting used to the idea of a new father and a new self. At times, she wondered where he was and why he didn't care enough to come look for her. At times, she felt angry all over again with her mom. Now it was time to break the news to her friends.

It was Crystal's turn to host *Shield* Night. Cameron came close to skipping the "Money Train" episode she was dying to see because she couldn't stand Crystal's mutant older sister. Neither could Amanda. Nor P. They'd met her once, at Crystal's Friday the 13th Sweet Thirteen birthday party, and that was enough. But they had no choice, knowing how Crystal would've reacted had they not let her play hostess. Being back in her old neighborhood was a little sad, but Cameron was excited to feel like she was home again.

Cameron arrived first, carrying a six-pack of Vanilla Coke, and climbed the stairs of the Stericks' brownstone with dread. She thought Crystal's parents, Zenstar and Wishbone, were really weird and her sister, Chimera, really weirder. Her knock was answered by Chimera, who opened the door, looked at her without a word, and walked away. The father, Wishbone, a performance artist, was away, apparently dangling upside down at a Williamsburg gallery for his One-Naked-Man art show.

Cameron closed the door behind her. The sisters were arguing over the television.

Crystal's mother, Zenstar, raised a star-speckled baton and struck the Peace Gong hanging from the kitchen ceiling, causing a painful boom in Cameron's ears.

"Chimera, harsh words damage your aura and gather darkness. Your sister gets the TV because she's having friends over. That's it."

"Shove it," barked Chimera, and stormed out.

A short while later, Amanda knocked lightly, holding a grocery bag in one arm. P held another. Between them there were enough snacks to bloat an entire movie audience. Popcorn and pretzels, M&M's and malt balls, and two gallons of ice cream.

Crystal opened the door.

Amanda whispered, "She here?" P waited warily for the response.

"Uh-huh," said Crystal. "Cam! It's them!"

"Not Cam," said Amanda, "your sister."

"Oh, her! No, thank God. I think she ran away from home again."

"Great!" said Amanda. "Oops, sorry. My bad."

"It's okay," said Crystal with a shrug. "She's so kryptonite."

"*Green* kryptonite," added P.

The girls got comfortable in the living room, talking and

pouring snacks on paper plates, filling mugs with soda, and scooping mounds of ice cream into plastic bowls. Through *The Shield* they crunched and munched, guzzled and slurped. Cameron watched the show with less attention than usual, her mind elsewhere.

Amanda finally said what the others were thinking.

"You seem bummed, Cam, what's up? Premenstrual blues?"

Cameron bit her thumbnail. How should she put it? What if they freaked out, these friends who were like sisters? Amanda was smart, she'd be cool with it. As for P, she *had* "gone black" once. And Crystal, she could be so bugged there was no telling how she might react.

"Okay . . . this is like *really* hard for me . . ."

As if on cue, Crystal's mother appeared, barefoot and swathed in a star-print, floor-length meditation dashiki. She did her prayer hands and solemnly nodded to the girls on her way to the kitchen. Crystal mumbled something about having embarrassing parents. Mrs. Sterick took a carrot from the refrigerator and retraced her light-footed steps. They focused on Cameron again.

"If this is about you living in the projects," said Amanda, "we're solid with you, right, guys?"

P and Crystal nodded.

Cameron sighed heavily. "It's not that." She felt tired all at once. "I found out that I'm—"

"Gay!" blurted out P. "Gallstones finally got to you!"

"Right," said Cameron, "speak for yourself. Now *listen*, this is serious, and it's kinda trippy. My mom had . . . I'm . . . My father was, I mean is . . . black."

The announcement drew snickers.

"Shut *up!*" squawked Crystal. "Get *out!* That's *craaazy!*"

"My ass," said P.

Amanda laughed. "You're joking, right?"

The expression on Cameron's face silenced them. Whos, whats, whens, hows, and whys tumbled in rapid succession. No, her mother wasn't in touch with him. No, they hadn't been together long. No, she never suspected anything. Yes, he was cute. Like a tide, questions and answers ebbed and flowed.

"Not for nothing, but what does that make you?" asked P.

The very question on all their minds. Was their best friend for so long suddenly someone—or something—else?

"Biracial, according to my mom."

The room was quiet. Cameron watched them squirm and make weird eye contact with each other. The lightness of her conversations with Sage and her mom was gone. She felt heavy and her stomach hurt. She thought about going home immediately.

Amanda spoke up. "Oh, why bother with that, it sounds so complicated. Just be black, it's cool."

"I don't think it's right," objected Crystal, "to tell somebody white to up and switch to being black."

That evoked a disdainful *"dah"* and a long *"hellooo!"*

"But I'm not black . . . not just black. I'm mixed. My mom counts too, you know."

Crystal said people were either black or white and that was it.

Cameron disagreed. "That's not true though. I found a lot of information on the Internet about people like me, famous ones too. There's Halle Berry and Tiger Woods and Alicia Keys and Ben Harper and Lenny Kravitz . . ."

". . . and The Rock," chimed in Amanda, ". . . and Bob Marley and the black Spice Girl, and that *gorgeous* tennis player, James Blake . . ."

Crystal stuck to her position. "But they're all black. I mean, they look black. And you're white-looking. So for me, I'm sticking with you being white."

"Crystal's got a point for once," observed P. "Not for nothing, but suppose the cops stop you for, I don't know, drinking in public. That happened to me once. All right, twice. But it was just beer. So they were like, *you* can go . . . to *me*. But the black girl with me, she got a summons. I know Professor Amanda says race goes by the parents but I think in the real world it's about how you look. It's like age—if you look young, you *are* young. Take my mother, she's thirty-nine but all wrinkled from suntanning. She *looks* a hundred now, so she *is* a hundred."

"Yeah, well, I don't have to worry about that because black don't crack." Cameron laughed weakly, and alone. "And I'm biracial whether anyone else sees it or not."

"But what's the *point* of changing who you are *now*, after fifteen years?" asked Crystal. "Anyway, *real* black people aren't gonna think you're black, so why try to be something you're not?"

Amanda answered for Cameron. "Earth to Crystal. You so get an A for IQ—Ignorant Question. Cam's not *changing* anything, thankyouverymuch. She *discovered* what she already is."

The vibe in the room was off. Cameron was glum. "I just need to know if you guys still love me, both halves of me."

"Of course we love you!" said all three. They leapt on top of Cameron in a joyful commotion of kissing, hugging, and tickling. With tangled legs and flailing arms they squirmed and twisted on the worn sofa like children at a pajama party.

The bus back to the projects took way too long and reminded Cameron how far away from her world and old friends she had moved. Her mother was waiting up for her, anxious. Marcus Garvey Gardens at night wasn't the most reassuring place.

"How was it?" Patricia had been making notes for a nail art workshop she'd been asked to give. "Did you like the show? What'd they say about you being . . . ?" She didn't finish her sentence.

"I couldn't really get into the show because of stressing about what I was going to say and how to say it. It got weird. It was like I'm not the girl they thought I was. Crystal wants me to stay white, Amanda said just be black, and P brought up prejudiced cops. It was a bummer, really. I wish sometimes that everything would just be how it was."

Patricia didn't let on how surprised she *wasn't* by their reaction. For chrissakes, it was a little hard for *her*, and she was the mother. She would never say it, but the fact was she'd raised a white daughter who no longer thought of herself as white. In a way, she too wished things had stayed the way they were.

"They'll come around, hon, it'll just take some getting used to. You're still best friends."

About that, Cameron was starting to wonder.

The school year was swirling to a close. High school seniors across Brooklyn were frenzied with plans for rented tuxedos, pricey gowns, gaudy corsages, and stretch limousines. At Herbert Hoover they flashed bulky graduation rings and boasted about their future colleges. Those going directly into jobs or trainee programs bragged loudest, salary-proud and school-free.

But for sophomores it was the usual year-end ordeal of test scores and report cards. Prompted by P, the friends agreed to form a study group. P's behavior, rather than her ability, dragged down her average. Amanda was the star and didn't need a group. Crystal did well without working too hard. Cameron was the one most in need, her grades fluctuating with her emotional struggles. Every week, they met, studied together, and quizzed one another. Cameron noticed that either it never came up or the topic of her new identity was being carefully avoided. Like, what was *that* about? If one of them said the word "black" in reference to anything—a kid, a singer, black humor, or whatever—someone else would shut her up with a look or an elbow. Crystal took a lot of elbows. Maybe they weren't doing it on purpose, but they were acting different toward her. That so sucked. Crystal might have been right, maybe she *should've* stayed white.

The test scores came out, holding no surprise. Amanda aced everything and remained number one. Crystal came in a close second. Hardworking bad girl P was happy not to have failed anything. And Cameron continued her downhill slide, which landed her once again in the hot seat of the guidance office.

eleven

The day was hot enough for the conservatively dressed counselor to be in a short-sleeved shirt. He wore a tie, but no jacket.

"Cameron! Miss Storm, good to see you."

She didn't understand why she was there. No teacher had written her up, and she'd been getting to school on time.

"What'd I do, Mr. Siciliano? Am I in trouble?"

"Quite the contrary, my friend. Pull up a chair."

She watched him reading a file marked "Storm, Cameron A."

"Good, good, you've really turned things around for yourself, kid. Your punctuality has greatly improved, even with the commute. As for your grades, well, they seem to follow the course of a roller coaster, up and down, up and down. The end-of-the-year test scores could be much better, but your earlier work shows that you *can* do it."

His manner was easy and he seemed pleased.

"Overall, I see a marked improvement. I wanted to personally commend you for a job well done, all things considered. I know you've had some . . . challenges . . . this year, but you seem to be handling them like a trouper. Life can and will throw us a curveball from time to time. The key is resilience, rising like the phoenix from the ashes."

The only Phoenix she knew was in Arizona, but what she *did* understand was that Mr. Siciliano was complimenting her. And that brought a grin of relief and pride.

"Yeah, it's been *most definitely* a . . . what does Mr. Robinson say? . . . *annus horribilus.*"

"Yes! Quite horribilus, I'd say. So," he paused, "how's project life? Not all that bad, I hope."

"Me and my mom, we're doing okay. Getting more used to things. She has friends in our building and can walk to her job, which saves money, so it's pretty cool."

"And what about Cameron, is it pretty cool for her?"

"Yep, sure. Haven't made too many friends yet, but now that summer's here I'm sure I will. I hope."

"And as far as being"—he lowered his voice as if sharing a secret—"white in a black neighborhood?"

"I'm not white."

The guidance counselor contemplated her in silence for so long that she began to squirm.

When at last he spoke, he said, to her surprise, "I know."

"What? But how'd you . . . ?"

"I'm biracial too, that's how."

The Godson was biracial! Whoa. She looked at him as if for the first time and for the first time she truly saw him. The coloring, the features, the hair. Shyly, she began her story. The photo album, falling as if from a cliff, awakening in her mother's arms, all of it. He listened and he understood. He told her of his African-American mother and Italian father, how back when he was growing up in the projects there was no such thing as biracial. Black Is Beautiful was the slogan of the times and you had to choose the black camp or the white camp. He clearly wasn't white, nor did he meet the criteria for being "black enough." So he gave up and chose neither, opting instead for the easy way out—he claimed to be Puerto Rican. And as long as no one spoke to him in Spanish, it worked. But that choice left him feeling erased and untethered, as if he were nothing and belonged nowhere. A fraud, in a word. Ultimately, he said, he found the courage to resist the pressure of the "race police" to bully him into a black or white box, and to accept all of himself.

"It's harder for you, Cameron, because you're only now finding out, at fifteen. From day one, my parents were clear that I was made up of both of them. I didn't have to revamp myself right in the middle of the throes of adolescence."

"You *get* it, Mr. Siciliano, truly! I mean, here I am already feeling like a total mutant anyway and then out of the blue I'm this half-and-half mutant, like, whatever! I still get so mad at my mom for making me have to go through this *now* when she could've told me when I was a laid-back little baby. Plus, I was so totally scared of how my friends would take it, and then too I've been thinking if I go out with a boy is it automatically an interracial couple because of me? It's like, there's a million questions you have but who can you go to, know what I mean, Mr. Siciliano?"

"Definitely, and *how.*"

The counselor was the first person, besides her mom and Sage, who seemed to really understand. It was like the windows of a cramped room had been thrown open onto fresh air and sunlight. Cameron took a deep breath and continued excitedly, "But I found out about all these famous, cool, biracial people on the Internet—actors, singers, athletes! Like did you know Mariah—"

"Cameron! Cameron! Easy . . . easy . . ." He got her a cup of water. "Listen to me, do me a favor, don't get caught up in celebrity worship, no matter what their race. They're just people like you and me. Your value comes from one person, Cameron Storm, in here"—he put his hand on his chest— "not out there. Remember that."

He rose to his feet. "Here's my card, Cameron, I wrote my home number on it. Feel free to give me a call if you just want to talk. Otherwise, I'll see you in September."

"Thanks, Mr. Siciliano, thank you *so* much. Can I give you a hug?"

They hugged and Cameron flew down the hall.

———

The students in Sage Brown's multicultures class were studying one of her daily "Peruse and Ponder" handouts, an excerpt from what she introduced as "Hilton Als's exquisite little book *The Women*." The jeans-clad Harlem native had a nothing-to-prove attitude, due in large part to her Harvard Ph.D., which for both students and teachers conferred upon her a certain feeling of royalty. She was the favorite teacher of many, but Cameron had her own reason for thinking her awesome—their talk. The young teacher didn't make kids raise their hands to speak, wore cool T-shirts that said things like "Happy to Be Nappy" and "Give Pizza a Chance," and had everyone call her Sage. But what most of the students liked was that she stretched them intellectually with complex, thorny subjects.

The teacher selected a student to read the chosen passage aloud. Tobias Richland, wearing oversize everything and an American flag do-rag, did his banger strut to the front of the class, and his gangsta-lean against the blackboard.

"Toby, you might want to stand up straight," suggested Sage, a wry smile on her lips. "It's better for your back."

"Ain't no thang, Sage," he answered. He cleared his throat dramatically. "Ah-ight, young'ns . . ."

Boos and shouts of "Stop frontin'!" "Talk normal!"

He was unfazed. "Y'all need to listen up and be schooled 'cause I'm about to—"

Sage interrupted.

"Would you be willing, Toby, to just read the words that are on the page? Thanks."

"Yeah, sure, word to ya mother." He began reading. " 'One of the more powerful examples in contemporary literature of the black American author's fear of the Negress is *The Autobiography of Malcolm X*, where Malcolm X writes "My mother, who was born in Grenada, in the British West Indies, looked like a white woman. Her father *was* white. She had straight black hair and her accent did not sound like a Negro's." Malcolm inflates the part of her he hated, feared and admired—her whiteness—which propelled his career as a "militant" black nationalist. Even so, he could not help projecting his face onto his mother's: "My mother . . . looked like a white woman . . . I looked like my mother." ' "

"Very good. See, you *can* speak, or at least read, English when you want to."

Toby returned to his seat. Cameron bolted into the room. Sage called her over.

"You're late," she said. "Care to share?"

Cameron was still catching her breath. "Sorry! Me and Mr. Siciliano . . ."

"Mr. Siciliano and I."

"Mr. Siciliano and I were talking."

Sage's face brightened. "Hmmm, lucky you. Here, this is what we're working on." Cameron took the excerpt and sat next to Amanda.

"Okay, guys," began the teacher, "I want you to think for a moment about two questions. What happens inside of us when 1) we reduce ourselves to an *approximative* skin color— black, brown, white, red, yellow—that groups folks into a *specious* social construct called race, and 2) if we're mixed race like Malcolm, we then reject any supposed off-color piece of ourselves that clashes with a chiaroscuro world? Who remembers 'chiaroscuro' from last week's class on so-called primitive art?"

"Black and white!"

"Exactly, Amanda. So come on, people, a penny for your thoughts."

There was a ruffling of papers as students reread the handout. Some mumbled to each other, hesitant to speak up since any mention of race was always fraught with concerns about political correctness. Others had hardly understood the question. A few ventured opinions. A black girl challenged the teacher's suggestion that race was a false social construct. She needed to get real, said the student, real as race. Black people look black and get treated black, and anybody who looks white gets white-skin privilege. Not true, countered a white kid, citing the struggles his Polish father had finding work. Another said his parents were Chinese immigrants and that people should be happy to be Americans in America and leave it at that. A white girl argued that people could be green or purple or whatever, if they were nice the world would be nice back. A black boy commented that Malcolm X's early rejection of white people as "devils" probably came from his own self-hatred and rejection of his mother.

"Excellent comments, you folks are brilliant. A couple of remarks though. Regarding niceness, many nice black people and nice Jews and nice whites, for that matter, were beaten, locked up, and even murdered during the civil rights struggles of the sixties. As for getting real, I don't negate race as a socio-cultural fact. But in today's world of motley mutts and blended biracials, race as *biological* fact is questionable. So call me a racial deconstructionist, but that's my view. And just a final note about Malcolm. He got over it. The pilgrimage he made to Mecca, where he saw fellow Muslims of all colors—races, if you wish—was transformative, and he returned to the United States as a humanist, embracing all people. Enough from me. Anyone else want to share?"

Cameron sat upright. Signaling to Cameron to keep quiet, Amanda shook her head no. But Cameron's insides were dancing.

"I do. Malcolm X's mother looked white, and mine does too."

There were mocking grunts and a few *dahs*.

The teacher gave Cameron an encouraging nod.

"And even though he hated it, he was mixed because of his white grandfather. I'm mixed too."

"Mixed with what," snickered someone in the back row, "vanilla ice cream?"

Sage silenced the giggling and told Cameron to go on.

"I recently learned that . . . um . . . my dad's black."

A hush fell across the room. Amanda shook her head. Cameron felt eyes on her.

"Really? Fascinating," said Sage, looking warmly at Cameron. "Your personal experience makes your opinion all the more valuable. So what's *your* take on the different pieces that make up Cameron Storm?"

"This is totally new for me, and at first I was pretty tripped out. I don't have a big, brainy theory or anything. All I know is that I am a part of my mom and a part of my dad. The way I see it, 1 and 1 is 2, not 1. So that makes me two things, not one."

Sage smiled. "Bravo, Cameron. And I *love* your formula." She gestured to the others. "Thoughts, people?"

"Omigod, I would be *freaked* if I woke up black."

"And what's wrong with being black? I wake up black every morning."

"I'm sorry, but Cameron's not black. Nothing personal, but look at her."

The bell rang. Over the din of chatter and commotion, Sage said again, "Bravo, Cameron." A clique of bouncy-haired girls had gathered in the back and were looking at Cameron and whispering. Some kids gave her a thumbs-up. Toby looked right past her. Amanda slid her arm through Cameron's, and together they left the classroom and ended the year.

———

As summer began, Cameron virtually lived on the Internet, scouring Web sites, reading studies, browsing personal pages, and visiting her preferred site, a chat room for "The Racially Mixed and the Mixed-Up About Race." She saw little of the others. Amanda was pursuing extra credits as a summer intern in a vet clinic, P spent her time partying and watching episodes of *Maternity Ward*, and Crystal obsessively assembled five-minute home videotapes, written applications, and recent photos for the new reality shows *American Playa Hater*, *High School–Reform School Swap*, *Survivor Mississippi*, and *Psychiatric Teen Vacation*.

Cameron worried about her upcoming birthday. This was the Big One and it was *sooo* important. She was turning sixteen and had to have a Sweet Sixteen party, but who would show up? She'd always had her birthday parties in her old neighborhood. Sometimes it would spill out onto the sidewalk and kids from other blocks would join in. But now she lived in the projects. With no new friends there and her old crowd on the other side of Brooklyn, who'd even come? The thought of turning sixteen with her mom and an old woman named Elvira was so total loser.

twelve

The Storms were having company and had spent the morning vacuuming, dusting, and decorating. The living room walls were hung with pictures of elaborately adorned fingernails representing basic, freestyle, and airbrush design techniques. On a table at the window bottles of nail polish stood alongside tips, wraps, overlays, terry cloth napkins, and electric files. The kitchen counter was a snacker's feast of cheese puffs, salt-and-vinegar potato chips, buttery popcorn, chocolate chip cookies, and cans of mixed nuts. Soft drinks stocked the refrigerator. Radiohead was blasting on Cameron's sound system.

"Cameron, Cameron! You're gonna have to lower it, this is a workshop, not a party! *Turn down the music, hon!*"

Cameron lowered the sound of blazing electric guitars, and up swelled a neighbor's rap music thumping through the wall.

"How in hell are the girls gonna hear me with that noise?" complained Patricia, irked but not enough to risk asking the neighbors to turn it down. She tried to keep as low a profile as was possible for a Norwegian-American blonde in a black housing project.

"I can't wait to meet them," said Cameron, fondly remembering the women who worked at Madame Elga's.

They heard a knock and rushed to the door. Cameron was about to unlock it when she was stopped by her mother.

"Cameron, what have I been telling you? You can't just open the door without first checking." A rash of push-in robberies in the Gardens had left Patricia on edge. "We're not in the old neighborhood anymore."

She squinted through the peephole, then opened the door. In waltzed Elvira in a pale blue head wrap and a dark blue checkered shift.

"I *am* invited now, ain't I? I gots to thinking about this nail polishing class you was giving and I says to myself, Elvira, you best go on up there and see what's going on. So here I am. Hi there, Cameron."

"Of *course* you are. There'll just be a few girls from work who need some pointers. I'm doing my boss a favor."

"Hmmph! You be careful being all nicey-nicey to the boss. First they wants a little favor, then a bigger one, and before you know it, you're buck naked on the man's desk."

Cameron sprayed a mouthful of chips in a burst of laughter.

"For your *information*, my boss is a woman."

Elvira came in. "Like I *said* . . ." She eased down on the chair, her motion slow and heavy. She pulled Cameron by the elbow. "Turn around, let me see you." Cameron complied, mortified that some old woman was checking out her butt. "Look at you, no bigger than a minute. You know, sugar, I was your size once . . . in the womb." As always, her own humor cracked her up.

Patricia was showing Elvira a fiber wrap—how to do the nail shortening, shaping, and dusting; what went into the application of resin coats and layers of fibers. Something slammed against the door. Patricia froze, her alarmed eyes on Elvira's.

"Don't pay that no mind, it's probably some of these foolish-acting kids doing what they do best . . . acting foolish."

There was a drumming on the door. Cameron peered through the peephole and, recognizing one of the project girls from the diner, took a panicked step back. "Uh, Mom, maybe you should look."

Patricia went over to the door. "Oh, it's just them, my crazy co-workers. They scared the heck outta me."

In bustled Bambi Thomas, Kali Harris, Colleen Kim, and

Asia Preston, all project girls from other complexes. They met Miss Vi and crowded onto the sofa. Patricia was ready to introduce them to her daughter, but where had she suddenly disappeared to?

"Hey, Pats, how you be?" Bambi was the plump sixteen-year-old mother of a seven-month-old. Her ample bosom quivered inside her tight pink top that said "More Cushion, Better Pushin'." "Just so you know, that was *not* me being all loud and ignorant in the hall. Colleen was the one acting all N-wordish!"

Colleen rolled her green eyes, sweeping silky black hair from her forehead. "Keep my name out your mouth, Bamboozle, you the one don't know how to act. Anyway, Pat, thanks so much for having us over for some training." She shot a sly glance Kali's way. "Because poor Kali desperately needs some help . . . Y'all seen the lumpy globs of polish she smears on her clients' nails?"

"Ha-ha, very funny." Kali, a part-time college student, was new at the salon. She was slender and tall with soft, dreadlocked hair and skin the color of cocoa. "I've seen the pathetic state of *your* clients' martyred fingernails."

Bambi said, "That's the stone cold truth. Jackie Chan be *chopping* up some nails, *haaaiiiYAA.*"

Colleen held a finger in front of Bambi's nose.

"What'd I tell you about calling me Jackie Chan, *bambina*? Do I look Chinese to you?"

"Yesss!" answered her colleagues.

The color of Colleen's eyes came from her Irish mother but their shape was that of her Korean father's.

"Yeah, right, all Asians have Chinese eyes, whatever!"

Asia, ponytailed and in a torridly tight "Project Grrrl" midriff, was eager for class to begin. "Y'all's trash-talking is holding us up big-time. I got a date and need to be outta here by six."

Patricia couldn't have agreed more. "Asia's right, so let's get started. Help yourself to the snacks in the kitchen. Drinks are in the fridge. I'd love for you gals to meet my daughter, but she seems to have vanished." She called, "Cameron!"

A few minutes later Cameron appeared with bowed head, dragging her feet. She said "Hi" without looking up.

Asia narrowed her eyes. "Yo, ain't I seen you before?"

"Unh-unh."

Asia looked closer. "Yeah I did. You was with them girls who was black frontin' in the diner at Kings Plaza! Me and Kwanzi almost *fired* y'all up."

"Kings Plaza? Black frontin'?" Patricia looked from Asia to her daughter and back again. "Cameron?"

Cameron had a knot in her stomach.

"I tell you one thing," offered Elvira, "you ain't gonna find too many looking like Cameron, so if the girl say she recognize her . . ."

"Cameron?" asked Patricia a second time.

Kali said Asia was constantly recognizing people who were somebody else. "Remember when you *swore* that a client was Shakira and it wasn't even a woman?"

"Oh, f'git you," protested Asia. "He coulda been her twin, right down to the cleavage."

She realized, from the guilty look on Cameron's face, what was going on. "Wait, hold up." She pretended to study Cameron's face. "Nah, now that I'm really looking, it wasn't you. The girl had dark eyes and flat, white-girl hair."

Patricia's presentation got under way with a handout of samples of nail art: fishes in blue water, bowed palm trees, smiling dolphins, long-tailed devils, and American flags. She demonstrated on Elvira the use of stencils, air compressors, and fitting tools and dazzled them with nine-carat gold Dior and Louis Vuitton nail-tip jewelry.

Cameron listened from the kitchen, eating fistfuls of cheese puffs and popcorn. She didn't get what the whole fingernail thing was about. The science teacher said global warming was going to burn up half the world and drown the other half, which kind of made fingernails seem really minor. What was important was finding some new friends. So far, all anyone said to her was "Wassup" when she came into her building and "Wassup" when she left. That was it. As for Amanda and them, when they *did* get together *she* always had to take the long bus ride since they were scared to visit her.

And that was the pits. Anyway, the new season of *The Shield* wouldn't begin until autumn. No, she needed friends from around here. But who?

The end of the training session was signaled by clapping, whistling, and barking. Elvira headed home sporting leopard-print nails. Bambi left immediately as well, to get home to the baby.

Asia saw Cameron eyeing her. "So you know, right, that we was just messin' with y'all at the mall," she whispered. "Could you see us beatin' down some white girls in a white neighborhood?"

White girls. What if Asia knew she was black? That might help start a friendship. "Um, Asia, you know what you just said about beating up white girls?"

"Don't even go there, Boo," said Asia, checking her watch. "Like I said, we wasn't gon' do nothin' to y'all."

"No, I know that. Truly. I just wanted you to know I'm not like a hundred percent white. I'm half black."

"Lemme see," responded Asia, examining Cameron's curly hair, fair skin, and blue eyes. "Now which half would that be?"

Cameron frowned.

"Sorry, that was a joke. Hey, you trynna be black, more power to ya. God knows there's enough of us who be sliding by as white." She checked the time again. "I gotta jet . . . Dashawn's waiting on me."

"I'm not trying to be black. I'm biracial. My dad's black."

"So's mine, so hey, we got that in common. But I really do gots to go. I'm around here a lot though, so I'll catch you later."

Cameron felt like a total moron right then. At least Asia said she'd see her later.

Patricia was on the couch with Colleen and Kali. Cameron squeezed next to her mother, who said, "Funny, how Asia thought she knew you. That's happened to me too. She's a piece of work, but nice underneath."

"Yeah. We're gonna be friends."

"Really?" A shadow crossed Patricia's face. "You don't think an eighteen-year-old is maybe a little old for you?"

"Mom, I'm fifteen going on sixteen."

Colleen joined in. "Yeah, Mom, lay off. She's a project girl now anyway, she can handle anything."

"Fifteen going on sixteen," said Kali. "I haven't heard somebody's age put that way in a long time. Cute."

"Well, then me and my unproject self," said Patricia, "are gonna go clean up the kitchen while you tough guys bond."

Another conversation began. Kali was juggling night school and working at the salon, but she was determined to make it to law school. "I've seen too much crime in my time. When I'm a judge, they're going to call me 'Hang 'Em High Harris.' Prosecutors will send me flowers and defense lawyers will shudder with fear when they appear before Kali, the Hindu goddess of retributive justice."

"I thought a collie was a dog," said Colleen. "Bowwow."

"Watch it, China—oops, I mean Korea-doll."

Cameron was puzzled. "Not to be too nosy, but what are you? You sound black, you look white, but you *do* have Chinese—"

Colleen jabbed playfully at Cameron. "Next fool say a *word* to me about Chinese eyes is gettin' a beat-down! I'm a mutt, okay? Mixed."

"Way cool! I'm mixed too. I'm white . . . *was* white, then I found out my dad's black, so I guess you could say I'm part black, you know, biracial."

"Interviews cost a hundred bucks," joked Colleen, "but I'll let you slide since I see you got *issues*." It wasn't real complicated, she said. Her father was a handsome Korean, her mother, a lovely Irishwoman. They met on the street in Hell's Kitchen and moved into public housing because the rent fit a short-order cook's salary. Colleen resembled her dad and looked salad-bar Korean, while her brother took after their mother, looking white with a question mark. Their madly patriotic mother taught them they were American. Nothing more, nothing less, nothing other.

"So like, what do you tell people?"

"Amerasian, Korean, white . . . depending on who's asking. Now if something *ignorant* comes out their mouth about some 'Chinese eyes,' I grab 'em by the collar and say 'Korean, asshole, Korean.' " She saw that Cameron was thinking real hard about it. "So what's your story, how'd your folks raise you to deal with it?"

"Umm . . . well," a glint of anger on her face, "it didn't come up."

"That's the way to go, drama-free."

Kali said, "Know what, Cameron? I'm mixed too, exactly like ninety-nine percent of all black folks in this race-ravaged country. But I'm more than happy to be just a plain ol' black chile. Less complication."

Colleen took in Kali from head to toe. "Plain, yes. Old, *hell* yes."

They were still elbowing and jabbing at each other as they got up to leave. After the thank yous and goodbyes, Cameron sat alone, heavy with the feelings evoked by Colleen's question. Her dad would've raised her to be solid about who she was. Most definitely. He probably would've said, I'm your dad and you're mixed and that's totally cool, then taken her out to a little kid thing like the zoo or the circus. Instead, she had to find out a million years later after getting used to being something else.

As she ruminated, the race part began to blur into the secrecy part until it seemed like her mother had *made* Dante disappear by not telling her she was half black. But then she remembered that *he* left *her*. So no, there wouldn't have been any zoo or circus or helpful mixed-race talk. Just as her anger was shifting from the mother to the father, Sage's words came to her—*Trying to protect us, our parents do the opposite of what we'd want.* Was he also trying to protect her by leaving? Right. She pondered this on her way to the kitchen.

"You'd be a good teacher, Mom, I liked hearing about the nail stuff. The women at Madame Elga's were nice, but not funny like Asia and Bambi and Kali. I like how they're always goofing around. And Colleen's totally cool. *And* biracial."

"*Is* she? She's not white? Hmmm, now that I think about it, she does have Chinese eyes."

"You can't say that, Ma, it is so not okay. She's Korean and Irish."

"Oops, my mistake. Korean eyes."

"I don't think you're supposed to say that either. It might be politically incorrect too."

"Well, when you find out what's okay, let me know."

They ate dinner against a backdrop of grim news stories that sounded like a world's-end roll call for the Rapture. Sweeping wildfires and torrential floods, Avian flu outbreaks and African famine, civil wars and terror alerts, an abandoned newborn, a gruesome carjacking, a corpse in a park. But what jolted them more than anything else was a small local item.

"... the suspect ... Napoleon Quisby ..."

The face of a large-nosed man with long, dark hair and small eyes filled the screen. Cameron turned white.

"Omigod, that's *him*, the freaky dude on the beach!"

". . . Quisby, a fifty-two-year-old father of two, has been charged with endangering the welfare of a child and is being treated in a local hospital."

"That's *him*? Turn it up!"

". . . Dana Diamond spoke to the victims . . ."

The camera zoomed in on a pair of teenage girls in baseball caps, tank tops, and cargo pants.

"We was right here when this white man walk up like he know us, saying he in the game and do we wanna be in a girl rap group. But he ain't look right—right, Jazzie, he ain't look right?"

"Unh-unh, Rose, he ain't look right."

"Like he was all bummy, and me and Jazzie was like, nah, we ain't feelin' him—right, Jazzie, we wasn't feelin' him?"

"Uh-huh, we wasn't feelin' him at *all*."

"So he pull out some brews and we drunk 'em—shoot, they was free, so hey—then he be trynna get us in his jacked-up car like we was dumb like that. When he touch Jazzie arm like he was gon' pull on her or sumpin', we went *off*, straight up wildin' out on that sucka. He was like 'help! help!' and people was watchin' the whole thing *rollin'*—right, Jazzie, they was *rollin'*?"

"Yeah, people was rollin'."

"The cops could see we was in self-defense and busted that beeyatch."

"This is Dana Diamond, reporting live from Farragut Projects in downtown Brooklyn. Back to you, Chuck and Sue."

The news story put an end to dinner. The sauce congealed on the spaghetti and the meatballs grew cold. Patricia's hands gestured and her voice was loud as she warned Cameron about sicko strangers, chat room vultures, Internet predators, and a slew of other evildoers out to harm kids.

The thought of what could have happened at the beach sent an icy shiver down Cameron's back. Memories of the two men she saw that day returned, the father bouncing his daughter in the waves and that creepy crawler sitting next to her. She was going to be more careful, she promised. As soon as she'd cleared the table and done the dishes, she got on the phone and called her best friends to see if they'd seen the news. P was the only one who answered and was damn happy the nut job got his ass stomped in.

thirteen

Cameron was alone and thinking about food when the elevator jolted to a stop. She was in the mood for a ham and cheese hero with everything on it. The doors slid open and she stepped forward. Her foot hit concrete.

What the . . . ? Oh, *bummer.* The elevator had stopped between floors. It was totally hot in that rickety tin box and a gross roach was crawling on the buttons and another one down the wall. Double bummer. She pressed Alarm and waited. The metal grill marked Speakerphone was plugged with hardened chewing gum. BZZZZ! No response. Sweat wet her forehead and armpits. Where was the alarm ringing anyway? For all she knew, maybe it was ringing only in the elevator shaft where nobody but her could hear it. BZZZZ, BZZZZ, BZZZZ!!! She flipped open her cell and tried to speed-dial her mom but couldn't get reception. She tried yelling. "Hello! Hello! I'm like stuck in the elevator! *HEL-*

LOOO!!!" Project elevators were the pits. "Help!" BZZZZ! "Help! I'm stuck in this friggin' elevator! Anybody out there?!" BZZZZ! "Help!" Nothing. Tears gushed, ran down her chin, and melted into her "Leave Fear Behind" T-shirt. She slumped against the wall, indifferent to what might be crawling, holding her thumb on the alarm button. BZZZZZZZZZZZZZZZ!!!

A voice responded. "Who dat?"

The words were as sweet as one of Mariah's high notes.

"Omigod, thank you *sooo* much! It's Cameron Storm from 12-G. I'm stuck!"

"Ohhh . . . that white girl."

"Yeah, that's me," she replied, happy to be known, even if as "that white girl."

She heard a second voice, a conversation.

"What you doin' out here, Dashawn, and I'm in there waitin', hungry? You got my wings?"

"Yeah, I got the damn hot wings, girl. I came out the stairway and heard somebody yellin' that they stuck."

"Somebody stuck again? Who?"

"The white girl from the twelfth floor."

"Cameron?!"

Asia began kicking the steel door. "Cameron, you all right? It's Asia! We gon' get you out, don't worry!"

"Asia! Omigod!"

Dashawn proposed unhinging the door with a screwdriver so Cameron could jump up on the handrail, bang open the ceiling hatch, and climb out the top of the elevator. Before Cameron even raised her foot, she heard Asia shouting. "You crazy? What if she fall down the shaft and buss her head open like what happened to Pookie when he got stuck? Damn, Dashawn, sometimes you really puts the ass in dumbass!"

"Then f'git you, get your own white girl out! I'ma go eat."

Cameron panicked. "Asia? You still there?"

"I'm here, homegirl, I gotcha back."

She told Cameron to do exactly what she said—hold down Alarm and press real hard on 6 and Door Close at the same time. Cameron did exactly what Asia said and the doors banged shut, the elevator bounced down half a foot, jerked upward, then glided to the sixth floor, where the doors slid open.

"Omigod!" Cameron was panting.

"Girl, you sweatin' like a purse snatcher." She hugged Cameron. "Bump Dashawn and his nasty hot wings, let's bounce. And we *sho' nuff* takin' the stairs!"

Outside, Cameron breathed in the plentiful summertime air, Asia leading her by the hand. The bench faced away from the building toward Manhattan's skyline, a sparkling reminder of the world just outside the project's door. Sitting there were girls doing each other's hair and singing every song that came on the radio, and boys bobbing their heads to the beat and rating cars.

Asia stopped in front of them. "Unh-unh, somebody gon'

hafta make room for us. Y'all know Cameron. Well, girlfriend was locked up for *hours* in y'all's brokedown mountain elevator. Make some room for the Asian Queen, ya *know* this bench be where I receive and rule."

The boys gave up their spots.

"Cameron . . . Ja'Qualah, Boomshaka, DéWanda, Illnana," said Asia. "Now everybody know each other."

One by one they greeted the new arrival. "Hey." " 'Sup." "Yo." "Peace." Cameron said hi to each one and shimmied onto the bench between Asia and Illnana, checking out the glistening braids and flashy clothes. She heard Miss Vi saying, *Everybody get along just fine for the most part, seeing that we* all *poor.* Not *these* girls, thought Cameron. They sported fine glitter T-shirts, capri pants, stretch miniskirts, jeans with sequins along the seams, and designer sneakers. She looked self-consciously at her cheap red Converse high-tops and holey dungarees.

Illnana buried her hand in Cameron's hair. "Your hair nice and thick for a white girl—"

Asia said, "She ain't—" but was stopped by a tap from Cameron's foot. She was already an emotional wreck without bringing *that* up right away.

"—but *damn*," continued Illnana, "you needs to do something with it. You never got your hair did? Sit down here." She pointed to the ground in front of her. "I'll hook you up with some phat Alicia Keys cornrows."

She was getting braids! She sat between Illnana's legs and

rested her arms on the girl's knees. Besides her mom, no one else had ever done her hair. Yet she felt perfectly comfortable having it parted, combed, and braided into fine rows by a total stranger. Maybe because Illnana acted like she was just braiding a regular friend's hair.

"Ooo, I like doing *your* hair, it's soft but it hold the braid. Now when I do Asia's brillo, my fingers be all cut up."

Asia wasn't having it. "Girl, pleeeze, get off the welfare cheese. I got good hair too."

Sunlight glinted off apartment windows, a warm breeze rustled the trees, buses rambled, Mary J. Blige wailed, and on and on whirled Illnana's fingers, twisting and tugging. Finally, she sat back and regarded her work.

"Perfect."

Cameron wore the expression of an excited child. "Really?"

Asia ran her hand over Cameron's head. "Man, that *very ill* nana hooked you *up!*"

DéWanda caressed a braid. "That's *phaaat*. Why you don't do mines that nice?"

"I doubles that, Dé!" said Boomshaka. "She leave mine fuzzy too, like her mama's housecoat, but Cameron's is off tha *chain*."

"Anybody have a mirror?" asked Cameron, touching her head.

All five girls whipped out small compacts. Cameron marveled at her appearance. "Whoa. Way cool."

"I give you props, Cameron," said Ja'Qualah. "White girls usually don't look nowhere *near* right in rows."

Overjoyed, Cameron blurted, "But I'm black!"

They *fell* out. Cameron was *crazy* funny.

Asia had to call them out. "It ain't no joke. She *is*."

Cameron recounted the story of her father. She wasn't saying she was black like *them*, she was biracial. She said her friends seemed to change toward her but she couldn't say exactly how, it was just a feeling.

"They white, right? White folks scared to death they might be as part-black as some of us is part-white, and you're they nightmare."

Illnana said black people were cool with biracials and all that. "So the more of us there be, the better, even y'all *real* light-skinned sistas." She patted Cameron on the head.

DéWanda laughed. "What's that saying, 'Once you go black, you can never go back'?"

Asia finished the saying as she remembered it, "And once you go white, you never gets right."

They laughed hard, especially Cameron, recalling a whole different saying P had told her about going black and never going back.

Evening took on colors of pink and purple. Cameron listened to stories of being tailed by store security, never getting *no* play from yellow cabs, of shit jobs, broke elevators. Light left the sky and reappeared in streetlights. Cameron had to go upstairs. She thanked them *so* much, especially Asia for saving her. Waiting in the lobby, Cameron considered her new friends, so different, so much bolder and brasher. Their self-confidence, as though they had life under control, impressed and surprised her. Yet they seemed to have little going for them. Asia and Boomshaka had already dropped out of high school, Ja'Qualah said she was getting left back, DéWanda hadn't gotten her period that month and might be pregnant, and Illnana hadn't dropped out but bragged about cutting classes. Why weren't they stressed and worried about everything like she was? They even seemed happy. And were louder and rowdier than anyone she knew. She liked them, most definitely, but was she *like* them? No, not really.

The elevator bounced to a stop. A few people got off. No one else was waiting, so Cameron let it leave without her. No way was she getting stuck alone again. It returned empty, as if teasing her, and went back up just as empty.

"Been waiting long?" An older man in paint-splattered coveralls pressed the elevator button several times.

"Yep," said Cameron, explaining that it wasn't the elevator's fault. She just didn't want to ride alone.

He knew where she was coming from, he said. Sometimes he felt anxious too that some knucklehead punk might be crouched in a corner, but he had something for them, yes he did.

"I didn't mean—" began Cameron, but before she could

finish a group of cheering girls from the Gardens' basketball league and a young mother with crying twins arrived at the same time as the elevator. Everyone noisily piled in.

Cameron wasn't sure how her mom would take her new hairstyle. They were rarely on the same wavelength about stuff like clothes and hair and nails. It's not that she didn't care, she *did* want to look good. The problem was that what *she* thought looked good made her mom cringe, and vice versa. Usually.

"Holy canoli, I almost didn't recognize you . . . What'd you . . . Let me see the back."

If she didn't like it, too bad, thought Cameron, preparing herself. It was her hair and that's how she was wearing it.

"Gorgeous! You look like that singer, what's her friggin' name, she's black, braids like that, plays piano?"

"Alicia Keys," said Cameron brightly. "She's bi—"

"That's it, Alicia Keys!" She turned Cameron's head this way and that.

"Hellooo, *owww*! The human head only turns like so far."

"Nice . . . very nice . . . and so neat. You look like a civilized girl!"

Patricia wanted to know who did the braids and could they do hers.

"Illnana."

"Ill-*what*?"

"Illnana. From the fourth floor. But she can't do yours."

"No? Why not?"

"*Because*, Mom," Cameron giggled, "white-girl hair cain't hold no braid."

Over corned beef hash and sauerkraut Cameron talked passionately of prejudiced cabbies and suspicious store guards, mean cops and crap jobs, and white people's racial fears. Her naive—white—mother needed some serious social education. Patricia ate, saying "um-hmm" every so often. Despite trying not to think of him, Patricia was reminded of Dante "breaking it down" for her years back with the same fiery spirit. Cameron announced she was inviting her new friends to her Sweet Sixteen party. Patricia didn't dare object. After dinner, Cameron began planning, noting her ideas on a sheet of paper. The first thing was to choose the right music. Would the project kids get into her collection of rocker girls and crooner boys? Going by what she heard blasting from windows and through walls, no way. She had no money to buy new CDs but could always download from a cheapo site. But download what? She'd ask Asia. Food and decorations were being taken care of by her mom. What to wear though? It would be so funny if she wore hip-huggers with a high thong and a tight, sequined top to freak out Amanda, P, and Crystal. Maybe a cool mix, like baggy jeans without holes and a nice top. She moved on to the guest list. Of course, her main girls. They were her best friends no matter what. And the new girls too, of course. But she couldn't have an all-girl party. She was friendly with a couple of the boys at school but not enough to invite them. And Toby was a total mutant. The girls would just have to bring their own boys with them.

Summer seemed hotter in the Gardens than in Midwood and Cameron spent the days lazily. A late breakfast. Morning cartoons, her little secret. Phone calls. Listening to music. Reading. And hours on Internet social sites watching home-made videos and hanging in chat rooms. She had different profiles, sometimes making herself older, sometimes being white, sometimes being black. Her mother didn't want her having company "just yet" while she was at work. But mostly she hung out with Illnana, on benches, outside the grocery store, and in the community center. Whenever she brought up her party, which was constantly, Illnana promised to provide "homeys galore."

fourteen

A Volkswagen Passat pulled into a parking spot a few feet from the "Welcome to Marcus Garvey Gardens" sign. Cameron had been waiting outside, one moment sitting, the next standing, then pacing. She was wearing nice loose-fitting jeans and a sleeveless light blue blouse. Amanda, Crystal, and P were making their first visit to the projects, for her birthday party. They piled out of the car and charged.

"Sweets!"

"*Caaa*m!"

"Heyyy!"

The girls leapt into each other's arms, jumping around in a circle.

"Omigod!" shrieked Amanda, touching Cameron's braids. "Your hair!"

"It's so . . . ethnic," said Crystal.

"*We* call it ghetto fabulous," joked Cameron.

"Well, go, girl," responded P, "and happy birthday!"

"Happy birthday to you!" sang the trio. "Happy birthday to you!"

The four friends linked arms and hugged. It felt like they'd never been apart. Cameron realized she'd been paranoid—they hadn't changed, they were still the best friends ever. From the bench Ja'Qualah and another girl were watching. "Stop lyin', Ja'Qualah," said the girl, "that child ain't got a speck of black."

The Passat pulled away so quickly it seemed to speed off, the driver waving from the window. Amanda's cousin could've stayed for the party, said Cameron upon learning who it was. P glanced at Amanda, who cut a look toward Crystal.

"Oh, she's too old," said Amanda quickly. "So where's the *paaarty*?"

"Yeah," said P, "I'm ready to get my dance on!"

Cameron and Amanda walked together. Dropping behind, Crystal whispered, "How're we gonna get outta here, P?"

The elevator stopped several times before arriving at the twelfth floor. Crystal complained under her breath that it must've been the local. P told her to suck it up. Then Crystal mumbled something about Cameron's hair looking totally black.

"What?" asked Cameron, hearing "black."

Amanda kicked Crystal's foot. "Crystal and I were saying we're happy to be *back* . . . together."

"Happy Birthday" balloons floated on the ceiling and "Sweet Sixteen" streamers dressed up the walls. The living room had been transformed into a dance floor ringed by chairs. Cameron's tour of the small apartment didn't take long. The projects were kind of fun, she said, leading them to her room. Sprawled on the floor, they shared stories. Amanda's boss had offered to hire her as his assistant after graduation but she was like, not *really*. She planned to have her *own* assistant when she was the vet. Besides, she had the gross feeling he had a creepy crush on her. But speaking of crushes, there was this really cute boy who came to the office whose Maltese kept biting out its stitches. As for Crystal, she swore she'd never get over how hurtful it was that her video had been rejected by every reality show, but she was going to set up a subscription video blog where people would pay to see her recite poetry. P was in a group for teens with alcoholic parents. And had herself stopped drinking . . . mostly. And she'd met this guy from the group, but he had a really big butt so she wasn't sure. Cameron mentioned as casually as she could that one of those girls they'd seen at the diner was coming to her party. What girls? The black project girls who were gonna kick their butts.

"No!"

"My ass!"

"Get *out!*"

Cameron reassured them her girl Asia was cool.

"Your *girl*?!"

"You're shitting me!"

"That's *craaazy!*"

People were arriving. Cameron jumped up. Amanda, P, and Crystal were introduced to Ja'Qualah, Boomshaka, Dé-Wanda, and Illnana. Much to their relief, Asia wasn't there yet. There were hellos, wassups, and happy birthday girlfriend. Patricia handed out cold drinks and cookies. The group stood together munching while Cameron told her stuck-in-the-elevator story. Crystal slipped over to the CD player and put on Marilyn Manson. Tossing her hair and stamping to the music, Crystal was in her own world. DéWanda bit her lip not to laugh. No one else moved, and as soon as the song was over, Cameron put on Asia's mixtape.

"T.I.! That's my *man*," shouted Boomshaka, gyrating her hips.

"Boomshaka! Boomshaka!" sang Illnana and Cameron.

Patricia opened the door to another group of kids, this one all boys. A faint pungent smell hung in the air that she recognized with consternation.

"We here for Illnana's party," said a tall boy with tattooed arms and a peach-fuzz mustache.

"Who?" Patricia was confused for a second. "Ohhh, Ill-nana." She opened the door wider. "This is my daughter Cameron's party."

In strutted a half dozen black teenage boys, street-elegant in designer baggies, basketball jerseys, and diamond earrings. Cameron grinned at her mother, whose expression registered both alarm and amusement. She watched Crystal turn red and Amanda run her fingers through her hair repeatedly. Ill-nana introduced the boys to "the birthday girl" in a flood of instantly forgotten names. Patricia rushed over protectively, a large bowl in her hands. She moved from boy to boy. "Pop-corn? You guys want some popcorn?" No sooner were the guys inside than P was up dancing with Boomshaka, body swaying, hair flying, and one eye on the new arrivals.

"Oh *snap*, blondie can *dance!*" said Shamel, the one who'd spoken to Patricia at the door. He decided P needed a male dance partner and slid between her and Boomshaka.

Cameron cheered P on, clapping in rhythm.

"Rock, P! Rock, P!"

Crystal was alone twisting at the closet-door mirror, in-spiring a number of jokes. Amanda was adjusting the strap on her shoe when a boy with a goatee and diamond-studded grill reached for her.

"Hey, cheerleader, you here to sit down or get down?"

With a confidence starkly at odds with her dance skills, Amanda waved her arms and snatched her hips. By now, all the girls were dancing except Cameron, who was enjoying the sight of her assorted friends when someone said something to her. She had trouble hearing over the music.

"I'm sorry, what?"

The boy brought his lips closer to her ear.

"I *said* I hear you got that Halle Berry thing going on . . . You ready for some bona fide, hunnid percent brother?"

At first she had *no* clue what he meant. Then she did.

"Uh, no, that's okay."

She looked around for her mom. The living room was full of teens, most of them invited by Cameron's project friends. Others had simply followed the music. Illnana made sure that everyone met Cameron. Girls complimented her on her hair and asked where she'd bought her pants. Boys did all they could to catch her eye. She saw her mom near the window and nudged through the crowd.

"Mom! Isn't this something?"

"*That* it is, hon. I had no idea you knew so many friggin' neighborhood kids."

Her mother's ironic tone went unnoticed, Cameron was too thrilled. "This is awesome, thank you *sooo* much. Did you see Amanda dancing with that guy, omigod!" She pointed him out. "See the one over there smiling?"

Patricia saw him. "What's that on his teeth, braces?"

"It's called a grill," said Cameron. "He said I look like Halle Berry!"

A hand touched Patricia's shoulder. "Yo, popcorn lady,

you the moms, right?" Before she could answer, a short boy with close-cropped hair was pulling her to the middle of the floor. Cameron waved, "Have fun, popcorn lady!" Patricia broke into her trademark stiff wiggle.

Amanda and Illnana came toward Cameron. "There you are!" said Amanda, almost breathless. "This party is the best. Guess what? Demarco, my dance partner? Well, he just got into vet school!"

Illnana cracked up. "What?! De-*who*? Girl, the only classroom *Dwayne* ever set foot in is shop class at Rikers Island. His lies is so *tired* they need to be *re*tired."

"Oh snap, Amanda," said Cameron, "you've been so played!"

Amanda was blushing. "*That . . . !*" She shot him a dirty look but didn't finish her sentence.

"*Doooooor!*"

Cameron squeezed past dancers and looked through the peephole. There was Asia and her boyfriend along with Kali, Colleen, and a guy Cameron didn't recognize, already dancing in the hallway.

"Happy birthday, girlfriend!" said Asia. "I'm feelin' your music." She'd brought her boyfriend. "You remember Dashawn, the one who *di'en't* help get you out the elevator."

Colleen handed Cameron a birthday card. "Hey, Sweet Sixteen, have a happy. Abdullah, this is Cameron. Cameron, Abdullah."

Kali gave her a bag. "For Birthday Girl. No more 'going on' sixteen." She kissed Cameron's cheek.

As the second wave merged into the party, Cameron took the present to her bedroom. A sudden movement frightened her.

"Crys! What're you doing in *here*? I thought you were mirror-dancing."

Crystal was chalk white. "I saw that girl at the door, the project girl . . ."

Cameron snatched her by the arm. "Stop being a baby. Come on!" She led Crystal to the living room and planted her directly in front of Asia, who was chatting with P and Shamel.

"Asia, this is my friend Crystal."

Asia leaned in close and glared. "Wassup, *cow*girl?"

Crystal took a step backward.

"I'm just playin' wicha," said Asia, bursting out laughing at the look on Crystal's face. She turned to Cameron. "Girl, please tell me that ain't your ma booty-dancing with Li'l Man. She is so busted."

Mariah Carey's funky hit was blasting. "I came . . . to have a *pahtay*," she sang, boosting the party's energy like a shot of adrenaline. Boys were poppin' and lockin' and girls rolled their stomachs like belly dancers. Cameron was admiring the dancers when two boys got her in a sandwich, one in front, the other in back. Her first impulse was to slip away, but she wasn't fifteen anymore. So she bounced to the beat, smoothly turning to face one, then the other. They smelled of cologne and sweat, and their strong hands held her waist. The feeling was weird . . . and she liked it. P joined them, shimmying in between Cameron and Shamel, Illnana pressed herself against them, someone else against her, and soon about ten teens formed a train powered by Mariah's beats. It grew almost too hot to breathe and Cameron twisted away from the group for air and water. The girls gathered in a corner were cackling. At the window Kali was questioning Colleen's boyfriend.

"Abdullah, huh? I thought you were African-American."

Colleen groaned. "Here we go."

"I *am*." He broke into an Usher move that slid into a Michael Jackson moonwalk. "Like collards and ribs, baby."

Kali sarcastically asked, "Then what's up with that name? I bet it's not from your mama."

Colleen moaned. "There she goes."

"There I go *where*? It's a valid question, right, Cameron, isn't it a valid question?"

Cameron's mouth was full of water. She nodded her head, trying to swallow faster.

"Aha!" said Kali triumphantly. "Even the birthday girl agrees."

"All right, sister, my slave name's Leroy Williams but my African name is Abdullah Jaheem."

Kali imitated the sound of a bell. "*Dong!* Wrong. 'Abdullah' is Arabic, not African. And the name 'Jaheem' was probably invented by the same California brother who gave gullible black folks Kwanzaa, which is *also* not African. You're the weakest link, goodbye."

"Lighten up, Judge Hatchet," exclaimed Abdullah. "This supposed to be a party."

"Yes! So let's go party," said Colleen, laughing and pulling him away. "And *you*, Lassie," she said with a chuckle, rolling her eyes, "watch ya back."

Cameron and Kali picked from the mound of mostly untouched carrot sticks and stabbed squares of cheese with a toothpick.

"So, Birthday Girl, you feel any different? When I turned sixteen, which *wasn't* that long ago, I thought I was all grown up and understood everything."

Understanding *nothing* was a better description of how Cameron felt. "My life's been changing so fast I don't even understand the stuff I used to understand, like family, friends, home. I guess I feel different about being me, period. But in a good way."

"Keep it good, Cam, because all of you *is* good, every little piece." A Missy Elliott song came on. "I love this! Let's dance, otherwise I'm going to end up with one of those BK soldiers in there."

Army guys were at the party?!

"No! You are *so* cute, Birthday Girl. BK soldiers are Brooklyn bad boys."

Cameron heard her name, followed by loud laughter.

"Hey, what're you guys saying about me? It better not be bad, it's my birthday!"

Kali said, "Don't diss Birthday Girl."

In an overly innocent voice, DéWanda said, "It wasn't nothin' about *her*. I said Cameron *mama* so old when she read the Bible she reminisce."

They howled. Cameron remembered a joke she'd heard in school.

"Okay, DéWanda, well, um, your mom's so confused she tried to put M&M's in alphabetical order."

Ooooo, crowed the girls, good one!

"Now, Cameron," said Kali, "you're a nice girl. I know you've been anointed Project Princess and all, but do you really want to sink to *their* politically incorrect level? 'Ya mama' jokes are so ghetto!"

"Oh no you *di'ent* call us ghetto!" taunted a girl with "Phatgirl" tattooed on her arm. "That's why *yo* mama so fat she had her baby pictures taken by satellite."

Ooooo . . . dis!

Cameron couldn't stop laughing. They were putting down each other's moms and not even getting mad.

Kali wasn't getting mad but she was certainly going to get even.

"Okay, okay, real funny. I didn't want to go there but you're *making* me . . . The woman who gave birth to you is so unbelievably fat that when she sits on the beach Greenpeace tries to throw her back in the ocean."

The laughter was out of control.

"So it's gon' be like *that*?" threatened Phatgirl. "What's your name anyway?"

"Kali, I'm named for the Hindu goddess of—"

"I ain't asked about all that." Phatgirl wobbled her head, a finger in the air. "Carly, or whatever name she go by, mama so hard"—she paused for effect—"that she got herded into the ring at the running of the bull . . . *daggers*!"

They were screaming and giving each other high fives. Cameron thought she saw a stung look flash across Kali's laughing face.

"Hey, then more power to my mama," said Kali, snickering. "*Y'all* are too project for us. Come on, Birthday Girl, weren't we on our way to the dance floor?"

There wasn't much dancing going on to Coldplay other than Crystal, her wildly waving arms drawing snickers and remarks like "What you doin', this ain't no rave." Cameron liked the song too and let her body follow the rhythm of the music. Clapping to the beat, Kali sang, "Go, Cameron, it's ya birthday!" Circling the birthday girl the teens picked up the refrain as Patricia appeared with a candlelit cake. The music was lowered and the birthday song sung. And to a thunderous chant of "Go, Cameron, go, Cameron!" Cameron Storm turned sixteen. She squeezed her eyes tight, crossed her fingers for more pull, filled her heart with a wish, and blew out sixteen candles with a force that could've swept clean a desert.

fifteen

The party had rocked its way well into evening and was winding down when there was yet another outcry of *"Dooooor!"*

"Hi!" Cameron said, flinging it open.

A boy stood there holding a small box wrapped in gift paper. He had light, odd-colored eyes and a soft bush of copper-colored hair.

"Hey, Cameron. This is from my grandmother."

She accepted the present. "Thanks, but who's your grandmother?"

He offered a hint. "Miss Hutton?"

Cameron shrugged apologetically.

"Miss Vi?" There was laughter in his eyes.

"Ohhh, okay, yeah! Thank you! I mean, thank her."

Rock music filled the hallway. He moved his shoulders to the music.

"The Killers. They're good."

Cameron grinned. "Yeah, I really like them too. You know, you can come in, uh . . . What's your name?"

"Ashford."

"Ashford?" It seemed like a weird name for a black guy.

"Yeah, I know. It's from Ashford and Simpson."

She smiled. "The Simpsons are like so funny, Bart and his mutant sister Lisa, omigod, they're like—"

He shook his head. "Not the Simpsons. Ashford and Simpson was a singing duo back in the day. My moms had a thing for Nickolas Ashford so she named me after him."

"Oops. Sorry." She had wanted to make a good impression but *dahhh*. "Well, anyway, come in, Ashford. If you want." She picked at her thumbnail.

"Nah, it's cool. I'm not from around here. Don't want to be the odd dude out. Gotta get back downstairs anyway, I'm doing some repairs for my grandmother. Anyway, happy birthday."

He turned away.

"Wait!" she said, then couldn't think of a reason why as he looked at her expectantly. Knowing her face was red made it get redder.

"Um . . . how'd you know I was me, I mean, that I'm the one whose birthday . . ." Omigod, how embarrassing! She was acting like a total *fifteen*-year-old.

He laughed. "My grandma said to look for someone pretty as a little princess." He pushed open the stairway door.

"Is everything all right, hon?" asked Patricia, walking up

as Cameron was closing the door. "Who was that? Why didn't they come in? You okay? You're awfully flushed."

Cameron showed her the present Miss Vi had sent.

"How sweet of her. Who brought it up, hon?"

"Oh, just this boy . . . I think he's her grandson or great-grandson or something." The faint smile on her mom's face made her blush all over again.

"*Maaa, stop!*"

The music had been turned down. Everything to eat and drink had been eaten and drunk. The few people left were chatting, exchanging cell phone numbers, and checking the time. Crystal was slumped in the armchair and seemed to be dozing. Illnana and Amanda stacked paper plates and collected plastic cups. P and Shamel were in deep conversation. Cameron sat near them. P was negotiating a ride back home for herself and her friends. Shamel reluctantly agreed to take all three girls against a promise that it would be just the two of them next time. The party came to an end and the last people left. Cameron waited for the elevator with them, then skipped back to the apartment.

Sidewalks sizzled and leaves dangled lazily from their trees. Cameron's days fell in rhythm with the easy summer pace. Since the party, most of the kids in her building either knew her or knew of her. Most days she hung outside with her new friends, playing cards, listening to music, practicing hair braiding. Sometimes she hooked up with Illnana to shoot pool or play basketball in the community center. Evenings there was dinner and her mom's funny stories about work, then talking on the phone, reading herself to sleep. She felt content in her new life as a sixteen-year-old . . . pretty much.

Cameron knocked at the door with the praying hands.

"My, my, you back again? It's mighty sweet how you dropping in on me so much. You wanna eat something?"

"Uh, that's okay, thanks," said Cameron, craning her neck to peer past Miss Vi. "Oh, yeah, thanks again for the diary, I've been writing in it every day."

Now Miss Vi chuckled. "And you very welcome . . . again."

They looked at each other for a moment, Cameron shuffling her feet, Miss Vi eyeing her closely.

"Guess I'll get going."

"All right then, li'l bit." She patted Cameron's back, then, as if suddenly remembering, "If you see my Ashford downstairs tell him to bring me up my mail."

Cameron banged open the stairway door and flew down the stairs. The boy who had preoccupied her thoughts since the party was in the building. On the first floor, she caught her breath, slowed her stride, and wiped sweat from her forehead just in time to catch his attention before he stepped on the elevator.

"Oh, hi . . . Ashford, right?" Her chest was still heaving. She thought he looked pleased to see her. "You have to get the mail for Miss Vi, uh, your grandmother, I was just . . . I ran into her . . . and that's what she said."

After her first awkwardness, conversation came easy as they stood at the mailboxes not noticing who came in and out, ignoring the Tenant Patrol ladies telling them they couldn't loiter there. They talked about school. He really liked Brooklyn Tech, where he was focusing on computer science. They were both going to be juniors. And music. He was psyched about getting a ticket to check out Ben Harper at the Brooklyn Academy of Music. She would totally do anything to see Evanescence in concert. They agreed on the new Pearl Jam album, but he was not feeling Pink *at all* and she most definitely did not get the whole Snoop Dogg pimp thing. By the time they exchanged cell phone numbers, Cameron was seriously reconsidering a possible high school transfer. Brooklyn Tech seemed more attractive every minute. She didn't want to jinx things so she mentioned her new crush to no one except her mother.

"Miss Vi says he's a great kid, good in school, responsible, not a troublemaker. But for chrissakes, you only been sixteen for sixteen friggin' minutes and all of a sudden . . . Miss Vi's sweet, but have you met his parents? What kind of people are they? Have you two— Are you playing it safe?"

Cameron blushed nearly purple. "We're friends, Ma, f-r-i-e-n-d-s. We've met twice. Once in the doorway here and again by the mailboxes. Can't people be friends in this world?"

Patricia reminded her daughter that she wasn't born yesterday. And she had another concern. "Okay, you want my honest opinion? Ashford sounds wonderful, a real catch. But you know, hon, it hasn't been that long since you found out— what I'm trying to say is, maybe you might be moving just a little bit fast with the new friends, now this guy . . . It just gives me agita."

Once again, Cameron felt a faint bite of anger. She'd worked out in her *head* being biracial, but if she'd always known she'd have grown up *feeling* it.

"Whoa, what's the problem, that he's black? Well, let me remind you, I am too . . . *now*." Cameron stuffed that "now" with as much reproach as possible.

Patricia got the message. From then on she had no more criticisms of the "friends" and made a point of repeating to Cameron the nice things Miss Vi told her about her grandson.

Lobby meetings at the mailboxes gave way to hanging out on the benches, where Cameron introduced Ashford to her friends. But soon they were going on adventures that took Cameron farther and farther away from the familiar turf of Marcus Garvey Gardens. They walked all the way across the Brooklyn Bridge, a first for Cameron. They paid their respects to "the souls at Zero," as Ashford put it, stopping in at St. Paul's Chapel to see the 9/11 Memorial Exhibit, watching construction on the Freedom Tower, and drinking a soda toast to "the resurrection" at a nearby pizza shop. They strolled streets lined with trees in Fort Greene, where he lived in a pretty brownstone. They watched tennis matches at Fort Greene Park and kissed in the shadows of the soaring Prison Ship Martyrs tower. There was so much more to Brooklyn than what she'd known, and it was exciting discovering it with him. At the Paul Robeson Theater they saw a Free for Teens matinee about a black girl who moved from the projects to Paris and became a famous writer. She visited Brooklyn's tallest building, the Williamsburgh Bank. And along the way they talked—about her lost father and his remarried mother, his plans to be a computer games designer, her lack of direction, their favorite Web site hangouts, and whatever else came to mind.

Cameron had never had such a mega-crush on a boy. She was forever thinking about him, calling, e-mailing, messaging . . . She'd even dreamed they'd gone searching for Dante and found him working as a lifeguard at Brighton Beach. She couldn't keep her feelings secret for long and told Illnana, who said she was "fiendin'." The word made her wince. She *was* acting like a total meth fiend. So desperate housewife. She'd stop calling him, that's what she'd do. Let him call her.

"HRU."

How *was* she? A whole week had passed without a word. She wanted to ignore the message, make him suffer a little, but she was too happy to hear from him.

"K." Right, she was okay. Okay enough to check her cell and e-mail every two minutes.

"SOMY."

Of *course*, she wasn't sick of him yet. No way.

"NW."

He proposed that they hook up.

"A3," she typed quickly, kind of wishing she hadn't. Saying *anytime, anywhere, anyplace* was totally out of control.

There was going to be a huge African performing arts festival that afternoon in Fort Greene Park. Dancing, drumming, tons of folks partying on the Main Lawn. They could meet at the tower around three?

"KUL."

Cameron felt about as cool as a grownup in a myspace.com chat room. Hanging with Ashford alone was fine and she most definitely felt comfortable with him. People in the Gardens knew her story and accepted her. But how would she go over at this festival, with tons of "folks," which was a word that meant black people, and how would she feel? She no longer knew what she looked like in the eyes of the world because she felt so different. Did she still look white? Was she starting to look more black? Had she always looked mixed-race and nobody said anything? She was afraid to feel out of place, rejected. But she really, really, *really* wanted to be with Ashford.

People were everywhere, pressed together on the lawn, camped around the tower, perched in trees for a better view. She found Ashford with no problem, his mass of Afro the color of a radiant sunset. They found a spot on the grass. A blind couple from Africa were singing in what sounded like French. The crowd seemed not to care and sang out the one word from the chorus they knew—*Bamako!* The dancers, full-bodied women and lean men, stomped and leapt and twirled ecstatically. Cameron looked at the beaming faces all around her. Everyone was smiling, their eyes meeting other eyes, meeting her eyes, without flinch or recoil, seeing nothing but folks of every hue, color, and complexion having a great time. Cameron thought about how she had despaired about leaving the old neighborhood, struggled with her identity, dreaded life in the projects, how she'd even feared this most awesome festival. She smiled back at people. It *was* all good.